A MOST UNPLEASANT ANNOUNCEMENT

"Inspector Jonas Thackeray, of the Twillings constabulary," he stated.

"Now ladies," he began in a dry monotone, "as I have already informed those present—"

He was cut off in midsentence by Vi interjecting an apology on behalf of our tardiness. She was stopped by an eyebrow that slowly arched itself up toward the rim of the bowler while beady eyes glowered at her from beneath the brim.

"If you please, madam!"

Silence on Vi's part.

"Yes, well, I'll begin again then, shall I?"

A slight pause on the inspector's part while those questioning eyes surveyed the room.

"The body of a young woman," he began, "whose identity for the moment remains unknown, was found on the grounds of the estate in the early hours of the morning . . ."

Elementary, Mrs. Hudson

SYDNEY HOSIER

AVON BOOKS ◆ NEW YORK

ELEMENTARY, MRS. HUDSON is an original publication of Avon Books. This work has never before appeared in book form. This work is a novel. Any similarity to actual persons or events is purely coincidental.

AVON BOOKS
A division of
The Hearst Corporation
1350 Avenue of the Americas
New York, New York 10019

Copyright © 1996 by J. S. Hosier
Published by arrangement with the author
Library of Congress Catalog Card Number: 95-94911
ISBN: 0-380-78175-1

First Avon Books Printing: April 1996

AVON TRADEMARK REG. U.S. PAT. OFF. AND IN OTHER COUNTRIES, MARCA REGISTRADA, HECHO EN U.S.A.

Printed in the U.S.A.

RA   10 9 8 7 6 5 4 3 2 1

Acknowledgments

To Commander G.S. Stavert, MBE, MA, RN (Retired), Honorable Secretary to the Sherlock Holmes Society, England.

Also to the memory of Sir Arthur Conan Doyle, without whose genius in creating the original characters this book would not have been possible.

Sydney Hosier.

Dedicated in remembrance to Harry James Hosier.

Contents

Preface	The Hudson Collection	IX
Chapter 1	My Life and Times	1
Chapter 2	My Journey to Haddley Hall	12
Chapter 3	Mrs. Violet Warner	18
Chapter 4	I Meet the St. Clairs	25
Chapter 5	Partners in Crime	35
Chapter 6	An Out-of-Body Experience	42
Chapter 7	A Deadly Arrival	59
Chapter 8	Grounds for Murder	75
Chapter 9	A Private Conversation	89

Chapter 10	The Room Upstairs	104
Chapter 11	Mrs. Warner Comes A-Calling	120
Chapter 12	A Riddle Solved	145
Chapter 13	Goodbye, My Sailor Boy	161
Chapter 14	Confession	175
Chapter 15	Conclusion	192

Preface
The Hudson Collection

Mrs. Emma Hudson's first step into the nineteenth-century world of murder, mystery, and intrigue began, innocently enough, with a telegram addressed to her at 221B Baker Street, London. Her response to it, and the ensuing consequences, resulted in a career as a criminal investigator, which, in many ways, rivaled that of her famous and flamboyant lodger, Sherlock Holmes.

Although Mrs. Hudson later wrote a series of books about her exploits, I have found nothing to indicate that she ever submitted any of her manuscripts to any publishing house. Whether this was because she did not want public attention focused on her, as it had been with Holmes, there is no way of knowing.

Upon her death in 1917, her personal possessions were shipped, as requested in her will, to her only known living relative, Mrs. Maude Havelock of Harrowsbridge, Sussex, a distant cousin on her mother's side.

I have no way of knowing what happened to most of her possessions, but I do know that the manuscripts, as well as some memorabilia, were stored away in boxes in Mrs. Havelock's attic.

In 1945, Mrs. Havelock's granddaughter, Diana, married Harold Thompson, a sergeant in the Canadian army, who was at that time stationed in England. On her grandmother's death in July of that same year, Diana discovered Mrs. Hudson's papers—the Hudson collection—in the old woman's attic. Realizing that the yellowing pages contained more than simply memoirs of a bygone era, Diana decided to save them.

When she set sail across the Atlantic the following year to join her husband, the Hudson collection went with her. Diana Thompson, preoccupied with married life in a new land, stored the boxes in the basement of their suburban bungalow. And there they remained.

I first learned of the collection through the Thompsons, whom I had met through mutual friends a little over two years ago. When they learned I was a writer, they asked me if I would be interested in going through the reams of material in the collection in the hope of putting it into some sort of order for possible publication. As a great lover of mystery novels, I eagerly accepted the task.

In addition to the manuscripts regarding the cases in which Mrs. Hudson was involved, I came across personal letters, postcards, faded photographs, a number of small oil paintings of rural landscapes, and the aforementioned

telegram, sent by her good friend, Mrs. Violet
Warner. Unfortunately, there were no letters
between Mrs. Hudson and Sherlock Holmes.

In the editing and rewriting of Mrs. Hudson's first case, I have been extremely careful
to hold true to the storyline as she set it down
in her neat and delicate script. The only
change of any consequence I made was to the
title itself. I changed *The Murders at Haddley
Hall* to *Elementary, Mrs. Hudson*. I'm sure she,
as well as Mr. Holmes himself, would have
approved.

> J. Sydney Hosier
> Toronto, Ontario
> Canada

ONE

My Life and Times

◌~My name is Emma Hudson. My involvement in the tragic and mysterious events that I now set down on paper began with a telegram from Surrey delivered to my residence at 221B Baker Street, London, the date of which, October 8, 1898, is still firmly etched in my mind.

Had anyone prophesied that my autumnal years would be spent in the pursuit and apprehension of the criminal element within our society, I would have thought them mad, to say the very least. Yet, this was the position I found myself in until illness forced me into retirement and seclusion.

As to my early life and subsequent marriage I offer up the following information with the reader forgiving, I'm sure, my vanity in omitting a date of birth. Suffice it to say I was born in Portsmouth as the only child of Captain and Mrs. Roger Abernathy. My father was a captain for the Blackwell line and perished at sea, as did every member of his crew save one, when his ship, the *Albatross*, went down somewhere off the coast of Malaya. My mother's passing occurred but a few short months after word of my father's fate had reached us.

Although the medical profession (and I include a certain Dr. Watson of whom I shall later speak) would be quick to scoff at my diagnosis, I believe to this day her passing was attributable to nothing less than a broken heart.

I was but eighteen years of age at the time of this most unhappy event in my life and had it not been for William Hudson, the lone survivor of the ill-fated *Albatross*, I am at a loss to think what would have become of me.

I had known Mr. Hudson since childhood, for not only was he my father's first mate and friend, but it was in our home that he stayed during those times between voyages.

He was a man whose manner I found to be both pleasant and straightforward. And, I would be remiss, even at this late date, if I did not confess to having had a girlish infatuation for him.

Although a good fifteen years older than I, he reciprocated my feelings (quite discreetly, I assure you). A certain look, a knowing smile, or the casual brushing of his hand against mine; it was a known but unspoken courtship, and it caused dear Mama, I'm sure, much misgiving. Oh, yes, she knew, as would any woman. I believe the female of the species, unlike the male, has a certain insight into the subtleties of the human psyche, a sensitivity akin to that of a telegraph wire—endowed with an inherent ability to receive and decipher the silent signals being sent.

Monies that my parents could have used for their own creature comforts were allocated to the finest of tutors for me, thus providing an education well above my social class and, while she herself was quite fond of William, it was a match she would not have wished. While I can well understand my mother wanting me to improve my station in life, being young, impressionable, and very much my own woman, I'm afraid my view of the future was limited with eyes blinded with love.

Poor Papa, of course, hadn't the foggiest notion of my feelings. It would be fair to say that whatever observational skills I possess came from my mother's side of the family. A slight tonal change in the voice, a too-quick movement of the hand, the shuffling of feet or the flicker of an eyelid, all this and more to me was an open sesame to the hidden truth behind the spoken words.

These talents would later be honed to an ever-keener edge in the years ahead by my having the good fortune to observe, at close quarters, a man whose intellect surpassed that of anyone I had ever known. He has been described as being the finest criminal investigator in all England. Others have dismissed that claim as being too restrictive, preferring to regard him as the greatest master of the criminal mind within the British Empire. While I admit he did not keep close company with modesty, he would, when pressed, describe himself as

simply being nothing more than a consulting
detective. But I digress.

Three months after my mother's passing,
William Hudson proposed marriage to me. I
felt I was the most fortunate of women. For
not only was I to wed a good and kindly man,
but I had been informed by my father's solic-
itor that I had been left financially secure. Although I would not be so presumptuous as to
label myself an heiress, my inheritance was
enough to enable a newly married couple a
step up the first rung of life's ladder.

However, prior to my acceptance of William's proposal, I made two provisos of which
I was most adamant. One, if we were to be
married, it would only be after a year's time
of mourning for my mother had elapsed. Two,
I insisted William no longer take to the sea as
a means of livelihood. I knew all too well it is
those who wait onshore for their loved ones
to return who suffer the most. How often I
recall dear Mama gazing out to sea with red-
dened eyes, anxiously waiting for the sight of
a sail on that distant horizon. I had lost a father to the sea—I did not intend to lose a husband.

I was right in thinking that William would
readily accept a period of mourning, but I
must confess I was somewhat taken aback
when he agreed that life under sail would best
be put behind him. I suppose, looking back on
it, I should not have been that surprised. Noc-
turnal visions of my father's face and those of
his dead shipmates had haunted him since his
return to England and would continue to do

so for the remainder of his life. Although he spoke only briefly to me of the sinking of the *Albatross* and his subsequent rescue, I did over the years manage to piece together what had taken place during those fateful months he spent on the other side of the world.

The monsoon had struck with such a sudden force and fury that many men, my future husband included, were washed overboard almost instantly. Cast into a sea of thundering winds and towering waves, William was fortunate enough to catch sight and take hold of a broken spar. Clinging to it for dear life, he rode the churning waters for the better part of the night until the sea spewed the hapless body onto a deserted beach.

Awakening the next morning, he set about in the exploration of the isle. Scrambling up a rise on the north shore, he spotted a ship anchored in the bay with its crew of Malay pirates camped on the beach below. This uncharted isle with its hidden coves was, he surmised, used by these Asian adventurers as a base from which to sail out and strike merchant ships who sailed the South China Sea. Being alone and unarmed, he quite prudently maintained a secret and watchful vigil throughout the day and into that long night.

In the early hours of the morning, William surreptitiously made his way down the slope and around the sleeping and inebriated pirates. Quickly and quietly he eased a boat from water's edge into the surf and, with oars that delved deep and silent, made for open sea, pausing to rest only when both ship and island had vanished below the horizon.

Thus began four days and nights of endless rowing until, semiconscious and delirious, he was sighted and taken aboard the *City of Bombay*—a Dutch East Indiaman bound for London.

While mother and I were of course overjoyed by William's safe return the knowledge of my father's fate sent the both of us into a state of melancholia. On my mother's passing, my mourning for her was juxtaposed with the sense of excitement I felt with respect to my forthcoming marriage.

And so it was, on a bright and sunny June day, one year after dear Mama had been laid to rest, I became the wife of William Hudson. Light of heart and in a carefree mood, we journeyed to London by train on a twofold purpose. We intended to honeymoon in that city as well as to keep both a personal and business appointment with Mr. Albert Warner, a former seaman and boyhood friend of my husband.

Mr. Warner was, at that time, the proprietor of a ship's chandlery in London. He had written to William inquiring whether my husband was interested in entering into a partnership. This proved to be the ideal solution, for there was little opportunity for a man who had spent the better part of his life before the mast to find gainful employment on land.

I was completely enraptured with London. The reader will bear in mind that I was not at that time what one would call a worldly person. My knowledge of what lay beyond the

perimeters of Portsmouth was limited to those
few occasions when, as a child, I would sit
very quietly by the hearth while Papa, with
pipe in hand and a glass of brandy at the
ready, spun tales of faraway places and distant
horizons. Macao, Chunking, Rangoon, Man-
dalay—even now as I write, the rhythm of
those names that roll so easily off the tongue,
conjuring up mysteries of Far-Eastern adventures, still fill me with a sense of excitement.
This love of the unknown, to seek out what
lies beyond the next mountain, or for that matter, behind the next door, I can only attribute
to my father and the stories he spun round a
crackling fire in that dear distant past.

We arrived at our appointed destination at
the time agreed upon by Mr. Warner and, after
alighting from the cab, I stood back to better
observe my husband's future place of business.

I remember the store as being bright blue in
color. From within windows on either side of
the entrance, a diverse and goodly supply of
maritime equipment was prominently displayed. This, along with the sight of the estab-
lishment being so close to the shipping yards,
made it all that we could have hoped for.

The door to the shop was flung open by a
beefy, heavy-set man who strode over to us
with a welcoming smile, greeting my husband
most profusely and introducing himself to me
as Albert Warner. We were ushered in off the
streets and into the store where, after an inspection of the premises, an invitation was extended to visit the Warners' living quarters

upstairs. There, we found his wife had prepared a table for the four of us.

She was a Manchester lass. A pretty enough young thing with a sharp wit, a ready smile, and possessed of a figure (had I but Aladdin's lamp) I would have readily exchanged for mine. With forty years having elapsed since that first meeting, the passage of time, not the genie of the lamp, has complied with a reversal of that original wish—wherein that silhouette of four decades past is now proportionate to my own.

After the sale of my parents' house in Portsmouth, William and I purchased a small but comfortable home on Porter Street, within a short walking distance of the chandlery. It pleased me that we and the Warners did get on quite famously. And with business prospering, we were able to set time aside to travel the continent once a year. Our evenings were spent taking in the music halls, catching the latest plays, and, weather permitting, an occasional seaside outing at Brighton. Although neither we nor the Warners were blessed with children, I found my life a full and rewarding one.

Alas, I now come to a period in time on which I shall not dwell to any great extent. I speak of the death of my dear husband in his fifty-eighth year. God in His infinite wisdom had seen fit to release from its earthbound body the soul of the kindest man I had ever known, that he might sail once more with my father and crew aboard that good ship Eternity.

For the first time in my life I was completely on my own. But however deep my sense of loss and sadness, I was not one to wallow in grief. An income was needed to sustain me, and what better way, I thought, than to take in lodgers. As the house on Porter Street was too small to accommodate such a plan, I sold it, and together with the monies derived from the selling of William's share in the company, I was fortunate enough to find and purchase a two-story brick house on Baker Street located in London's West End.

The Warners and I continued to keep in touch either personally or by post, but as the years passed we saw and heard less and less from each other until it came to a point where not so much as a Christmas card was exchanged. It seemed at the time yet another door had been closed behind me.

The Baker Street house yielded a good if not steady income. Being a transient trade, lodgings were of intermittent intervals ranging from a fortnight to three months at best. I therefore thought myself quite fortunate when two gentlemen took up residence with the assurance their stay was to be of a permanent nature.

Finding the upstairs quarters to their liking, two bedrooms and a spacious sitting room, they moved in bag and baggage that same day. They had not been with me long when I found that the taller of the two possessed what I can only describe as a mercurial personality. I found him at times capable of short outbursts of temper, deep periods of melancholia, and the highest of spirits. The shorter of the pair was affable enough but subject to a vagueness of thought at times. Whether this was from his having sustained an injury at the battle of Maiwand during his stint as an army surgeon in Afghanistan, I don't know. In any event, they were a far more lively and interesting pair than previous occupants, for they had brought a sense of excitement into what had become for me a rather mundane existence.

The reader will have surmised, at this point, that I speak of none other than Mr. Sherlock Holmes and Dr. John Watson. Although there were advantages to having such a distinguished pair of gentlemen as lodgers, I must confess it took me no little time to become accustomed to hearing the wailing of a violin at all hours of the night and day, as well as to the odd odors that permeated the house from chemical experiments both gentlemen were prone to carry out on various occasions.

Over the years, Sherlock Holmes had obtained a certain standing throughout England and abroad by his solving of the most baffling of crimes, due in no small measure, I might add, to Dr. Watson's published exploits of his friend's most sensational cases. While I was mentioned, albeit briefly, by Dr. Watson in certain cases of which he wrote, permission to use my name was never granted. Although none was needed, I felt he could have asked out of common courtesy, as I would have done in the writing of this story had not the good doctor passed away a number of years ago. However,

this coupling in print of Holmes, Watson, and
Hudson was, in fact, the reason I received the
telegram from a woman I had not seen these
many years—Mrs. Violet Warner.

TWO

My Journey to Haddley Hall

〜THE TELEGRAM WAS a puzzle to me on two counts. The gist of the constrictive phrasing had been a request by Violet that I intercede on her behalf in having Mr. Holmes come at once to Haddley Hall in regard to a most urgent matter. Haddley Hall, indeed! Had the Warners' business flourished to such an extent over the years that they could now afford an estate? As Violet herself would have said, "Not ruddy likely!" Why then Haddley Hall? And what could be of such importance that it would require the services of Sherlock Holmes?

Due to the urgency of the message plus the fact that Mr. Holmes and Dr. Watson had taken themselves off to Scotland for a fortnight, I decided I'd set off for Haddley Hall myself the following morning.

My journey was an arduous one. I had taken the train to the nearest village and since my arrival at the estate was unexpected, for I had sent no return reply by wire, I was forced to look for local transport for the remainder of my journey. After stopping for a quick bite at a local tea shop, I was fortunate enough to find a farmer with horse and cart who assured me he would be passing Haddley on his way home. Since the old farmer was rather uncommunicative, we rode in silence through a Constable landscape of dusty, deep-rutted roads and rolling hills of muted green and somber browns; until at last encountering a fieldstone wall, which we followed a good quarter mile before arriving at a most foreboding black wrought-iron gate.

The fellow pulled back smartly on the reins, bringing the poor animal to a sharp stop, then, jerking his thumb toward the gate, I received a mumbled, "Haddley Hall." As no hand was forthcoming in helping me to alight, I climbed down as best I could and extracted my valise from the back of the cart. After a farewell consisting of no more than a slight nod of the head coupled with a cursory touching of thumb and forefinger to cap, the old farmer flicked the reins and together both man and beast continued their silent trek homeward.

I still had a good fifteen minutes walk ahead of me along a private road on whose sides were planted, at regular intervals, towering poplars in the Italian style of landscaping. As for myself, I would have preferred to see good, solid English oak. Nevertheless, footsore, weary, and covered in dust, I at last arrived at my destination.

Haddley was a monolith of simplistic design. Georgian, I thought, although I must confess recognizing varying architectural designs is not my forte. That was one area, I reminded myself, I would have to pursue more diligently on my return to London. Not that my parents had been remiss in affording me a proper education, but the plant of knowledge must be continually fed and I find a quizzical mind to be the necessary nutrient if it is to grow and flourish.

I pride myself in having attained a fluency in two foreign languages, a knowledge of historical data, an understanding of various branches of medicine, as well as an appreciation of the arts. I also pursue the pastime of painting; my attempts at putting oil to canvas, however amateur the result, afforded me many a pleasurable afternoon. However, I would be remiss if I did not confess that credit for whatever additional knowledge I had obtained over the years following my husband's passing, should, in all honesty, go to Mr. Holmes.

Having found himself at loose ends after the solving of a particularly trying case, he took it upon himself to while away an afternoon at my kitchen table, indulging himself in biscuits and tea.

After returning cup to saucer, the great man very solemnly leaned that sparse frame across the table and, wagging a finger in my direction, advised me in a stern, no-nonsense tone of voice that if I wished to add to my understanding of the world at large, "Then, I believe, Mrs. Hudson, my best advice to you, to paraphrase Shakespeare, would be get thee to a library."

It was sound advice that I was to follow religiously. Unfortunately, on several occasions, it led to some unpleasantness. I would, from time to time, be unaware of the lateness of the hour as I trudged home from either library, art gallery, or museum, and, on arrival, find Doctor Watson pacing the hallway mumbling and grumbling to himself about not being served his evening meal at the proper hour. Still it has been a worthwhile education and if the information acquired had all come to nought, the very fact that I knew what I knew would be sufficient unto itself.

At any rate, I found Haddley Hall to be quite impressive. So much so that I hesitated at the foot of the steps leading up to the entrance and cast a furtive glance at the obligatory stone lions on either side that I thought eyed me rather suspiciously in return.

On reaching the top, I stood there, hat askew, covered in dust, and looking for all the world, I'm sure, like some long-lost orphan waif, or at best, a poor relation come a-calling.

C'mon, old girl, I told myself, the next thing you'll be seeing is Marley's face staring back at you from the brass door knocker.

At that somewhat whimsical thought, I afforded myself a slight smile and reaching for "Marley" brought brass down upon brass. Timidly at first, then, since the deed had been done and no answer was forthcoming, I banged it quite vigorously a few more times and waited. The door opened and from behind that august wooden structure the face of an elderly and very distinguished white-gloved butler peered out at me.

"Yes?"

"I'm here to see Mrs. Violet Warner," I said, in what I hoped was an imperious tone.

A pause.

"I see—yes. Please come in."

He stepped back, opening the door further as I entered.

"If I may, madam?" His eyes darted back and forth from coat to hat.

"Oh, yes, certainly," I replied, feeling a little more relaxed as apparel and valise were whisked away into a side closet.

"If you'll be so kind as to wait here, madam, I'll inform Mrs. Warner of your presence."

I watched him silently cross the gleaming parquet floor, and although the step was sure and precise, I detected a certain melancholia. The shoulders sagged, not, I thought, from advancing age, but from a depression that seemed all-enveloping. On reaching a sliding door just off the entrance hall, he paused before opening it.

"I'm sorry," he said, with an apologetic smile. "The name again is . . . ?"

I drew myself up to my full five feet, four inches. "Hudson," I said. "Mrs. Emma Hudson."

The old gentleman nodded in acknowledgment before silently disappearing behind the door.

Well, now, thought I, the Warners have

come a long way, in more than miles, from the shipyards of London to a palatial estate such as this. But if this journey of mine was for no more than a lost article of some sort, I would be sorely vexed, notwithstanding the opportunity of renewing past acquaintances.

I was interrupted in my thoughts by the sound of the sliding door being eased back as the white-gloved butler with the sad but kind eyes reappeared. "This way, if you please, madam."

As I entered into the room, he stepped aside and silently slid the door shut behind me, leaving me alone for the first time in nearly twenty years with Violet Warner.

THREE

Mrs. Violet Warner

"Emma! Emma Hudson! I couldn't believe me ears when old Hogarth says there's an Emma Hudson here to see me, but where's your Mr. Holmes, eh?"

"It's nice to see *you* again too, Vi," I replied, in a cutting tone.

Her eyebrows shot up at my remark as blotches of red surfaced on both cheeks. She rose quickly from her chair and, being flustered by her innocent yet insensitive query, all but upset the tea service on the trolley in front of her.

"Oh, I am that sorry, Em. It's lovely seein' you again, it is, after all these years."

In an overcompensating gesture, she approached with arms extended and we embraced.

"Well, now, m'girl," said I, stepping back and taking her hands in mine, "I must say you look absolutely wonderful."

Although her face and figure had filled out

18

considerably over the intervening years and a few wrinkles had found their way into that saucy face, the eyes still retained their sparkle. And, I must admit, she did look quite presentable in her dress of taffeta, but why she chose the color green, I shall never know. It never was her color.

"Aye, and you haven't changed a bit either," was the smiling response. "You're just as I remembered. But 'ere, now, there's no need for us to be standin' in middle of room like a pair of ruddy statues. Sit down, luv. I've a fresh pot of tea I know you won't say no to—not if I knows Emma Hudson. Bit of sugar, no milk, right?"

"Yes, that would be lovely." I smiled, surprised and touched that she would have remembered after all these years. "Especially after eating dust for the better part of the day. But, as to our appearance," I continued, seating myself opposite her and the tea cart, "if neither of us has changed over the last twenty years, we surely must be candidates for an article in the *Lancet*."

"Aye," she chuckled, as she set about pouring my tea into a most exquisite porcelain cup, "we may have added a little more weight here and there and a wrinkle or two over the years, but as I always say, if you have your health then the rest is just so much water down the well."

"So much water—?" I hid a smile as she handed me the steaming cup. "Ah," said I after an enjoyable sip or two, "that hit the spot. But what's all this?" I asked, with an airy

wave of my arm, as if to encompass not only
the room but the very estate itself. "Don't tell
me you and Albert have—"

"Albert!" My old friend sat bolt upright in
her chair. "You didn't know? But that's right,
luv, you couldn't, could you?"

"Know what?" I asked, replacing cup to
saucer as I leaned forward in anticipation of
her answer.

"Why, poor old Bert's been dead and buried
these last nine years, he has."

"Oh, I am sorry to hear that Vi." I was both
startled and saddened by the news. "No, I
didn't know. How terrible for you. He was a
wonderful person."

"Well, he went quick, like. No sufferin',"
she replied quietly, looking down at her lap
and unconsciously smoothing out imaginary
creases from her dress. "He were a good old
soul, my Bert was—as was your William." Her
face blossomed into a smile. "And didn't we
four have some fine old times together! Do
you remember when we—"

At this point, I shall not suffer the reader to
journey down the private path of memories
shared by two elderly ladies, other than to say
that our reminiscing continued until the white-
gloved butler entered the study where he proceeded to light the lamps before silently taking
his leave.

"Enough of the past, Vi," I said. "You simply must bring me up to date. What on earth
are you doing here, at Haddley? It's apparent
you aren't one of the household staff. Unless,

of course, you're a long-lost relation of the St. Clairs."

That startled her. "You know the St. Clairs, then?"

"Only that they are the owners of Haddley Hall."

That was the only information I had been able to glean from the otherwise close-mouthed farmer who had driven me to the estate.

"My position, if you please, madam," Vi responded, in a comical Mayfair accent, while primping her hair in an exaggerated fashion, "is that of a lady's companion to Her Grace, Lady Agatha St. Clair, don't you know." Then, breaking out in a peal of laughter added, "It all sounds very lah-de-dah, don't it?"

"But, how in the world," I wondered aloud, "did all this come about?"

"Well see now, it were like this," she responded, repositioning herself in her chair. "It seems his lordship died in some sort of hunting accident 'bout the same time as did my Bert. Lady St. Clair was that upset with his lordship's passing, and all, her doctor prescribed a sea voyage to help take her mind off it, like. It was the duke of Norwall, him being a close friend of the family, who put his yacht at her disposal. And a right proper gent he is too. When he learns her ladyship was in need of a companion for the voyage, he suggests my name to her."

"And this—this duke of Norwall, how did he know of you?"

"Why, through the store, of course. The

duke did business with us, buying equipment, from time to time, as he did, for his yacht. 'Course now, he didn't come round all the time. Sometime he'd send his man. Still, he knew I was a recent widow meself, trying to make a go of the store on my own. So, he ups and arranges for me to meet her ladyship, and for some reason or other the two of us hit it off right smart. And it were such a lovely voyage. I can understand now, the feelings Bert and your William had for the sea. After we came back she asked me if I'd like to stay on here at the estate. Said I was the only one to ever make her laugh, she did. Though," she added, still somewhat perplexed by it all, "I never thought I ever said anything funny—but there you are, you see. So I sells the store, lock, stock, and barrel. And here I am. Care for another biscuit, luv?"

To say I was completely flabbergasted by the turns Vi's life had taken would be an understatement. Still, we both had had rough roads to travel at one time or another and I was glad to see my friend was now in a position to enjoy her later years in comfort.

"I'm so happy everything has turned out so well for you, Vi," I said—and meant it.

"Aye, well, the truth of it is, I won't be here much longer. On account of her ladyship, like."

"Oh, I see," I replied, with a knowing smile. "Had a bit of a run-in with her, did you? Well, not to worry, I'm sure she . . ."

"No, t'weren't nothing like that," was the hastily voiced interjection. "The thing of it is,

Lady St. Clair is dead. That's why I sent for your Mr. Holmes."

That stopped me in my tracks. "Dead!" I repeated. "Her ladyship is dead? But, surely you realize," I continued in what, I'm afraid, was a somewhat patronizing tone, "Mr. Holmes is a detective. Not a mortician."

Her eyes narrowed in on me. "I know what he flippin' is, all right!" she snapped. "Her ladyship's been murdered—*that's* why I wanted to see your Mr. Holmes!"

I was in the act of reaching for the last remaining biscuit when my hand froze in mid air.

"Murdered! Good Lord, Violet! Surely you can't mean that!"

"Aye. I mean it well enough."

Her eyes darted about as if in an overreaction to a fear the room might be harboring a hidden and unwanted visitor, before adding, "I saw it happen, I did. Sure as I'm looking at you. But you'll never get the St. Clairs to admit it were murder." Then, once more adopting an exaggerated upper class accent, she added, "Passed away in her sleep, poor thing. Oh, she passed away, all right. But it weren't none of her doin'. So, where's your Mr. Holmes, eh? That's what I'd like to know!"

"My dear, Violet, do stop calling him *my* Mr. Holmes. If truth be known, he and Dr. Watson at this very minute are somewhere up in Scotland, shooting grouse, or whatever it is they shoot up there. That's why I took the opportunity when I received your telegram to visit you in his stead. But there was no mention of murder in the wire I received. If there had been . . ."

I paused, mentally calculating what indeed I would have done. "I would have come in any event!" I announced triumphantly, quite pleased with myself that my sense of adventure had not left me. "Now then," I continued, "out with it, m'girl. Tell me everything you know." It was exactly what Mr. Holmes would have said, I'm sure, under the same circumstances.

She studied me quietly for a few moments, no doubt wondering whether the woman opposite her, who had just walked into her life after all these years, was the one to entrust with what knowledge she had of Lady St. Clair's death. Evidently I passed the test. She began her story.

"Well, in the first place, you're right," she said, while absentmindedly rubbing a finger over the rim of her now empty cup. "I never did mention the word murder, bein' as how you never know who's goin' to be reading the telegram before it ends up with the person you sent it to. As for seein' her ladyship bein' done away with—"

She stopped, tilting her head to one side like a bird sensing an unknown danger. As her eyes turned toward the door of the study, I followed her gaze to see it being silently eased open.

FOUR

I Meet the St. Clairs

☙"OH, IT'S YOU, Mrs. Warner. We *thought* we heard voices in here."

A slimly built man, fortyish, with a slight stoop and a somewhat vacant manner, entered the room, followed in turn by a woman who I assumed was his wife.

"I'm sorry, I don't believe we've met," the man said, turning his attention to me with a voice as expressionless as his face.

Violet spoke up before I had an opportunity to reply. "Oh, excuse me, Sir Charles. This is an old friend of mine what's come down from London—Mrs. Emma Hudson. Em, this here's Sir Charles and his wife, Lady Margaret."

The man's deep, hooded eyes, set between a prominent nose, swept blandly over me. His hair, save for the white-flecked sideburns, was jet-black, slicked down, and parted in the middle. I wondered why, with the male's ability to grow a beard, he had not done so; the added foliage would have served to camouflage a decidedly weak chin and helped to balance out the beaklike nose. All in all, I'm afraid, I was left with the impression of a man possessed with all the personality of lint.

Lady Margaret was an entirely different matter. Chiseled features, upswept auburn hair—very patrician in appearance. No concave profile here. This, if I was not mistaken, was no power behind the throne, this was the throne, itself!

With her graceful and dignified bearing she was still a handsome woman whom I would estimate to be no more than a year or two younger than her husband. Looking at her, one could imagine a time when those eyes would have flashed and sparkled at the countless gentlemen who waltzed her round many a ballroom floor. The eyes now, I likened to her ring, a diamond: cold, hard, and brilliantly blue. She stood to the left of her husband in an affected attitude of boredom or annoyance—or both.

I nodded politely. "Sir Charles—Lady Margaret."

My acknowledgment was received with a wan smile from Sir Charles and a slight nod of the head from the patrician statue. There followed an awkward pause until Vi stepped in to fill the breach.

"I've asked Mrs. Hudson to stay on for a few days," she said, "being that upset, what with the passing of her ladyship and all. If that's all right with you, Sir Charles."

As the hooded eyes swept over me once

again, I detected a slightly audible but sharp intake of breath from Lady Margaret. Sir Charles glanced at his wife, who avoided his eyes by staring at some imaginary spot on the ceiling. Putting a hand to his mouth, he coughed nervously a few times before answering.

"Well—that is—yes, of course, Mrs. Warner. I'll have one of the servants take whatever luggage Mrs. Hudson has brought, up to—ah, let's see, I believe the room at the end of the upstairs hall would be—"

"If you don't mind, Sir Charles," interrupted Vi, "I thought Em, Mrs. Hudson, that is, might stay with me in my room, like."

What's this? I wondered. Vi, wanting me in her room? Was she actually afraid for herself? Was it the St. Clairs whom she believed we must be on guard against?

The baronet of Haddley merely shrugged his shoulders in response. "Whatever you wish, Mrs. Warner," he replied on walking toward the far end of the room.

We watched in silence as he proceeded to pour himself a large brandy. While I am not one to indulge in alcoholic beverages, at least, not to any great extent, I would not have turned down an offer of a sherry, should one have been extended. At this point, the matriarch of the manor spoke for the first time since entering the study. "You do realize, do you not, Mrs. Warner, that with the death of her ladyship, your services will no longer be required."

The cutting edge to her voice and the way she avoided looking directly at Vi as she spoke left me with the impression that Lady Margaret found the very act of speaking directly to a "social inferior" to be quite distasteful.

"You may, if you wish," she continued on, "stay on until the end of the week—giving you enough time, I'm sure, to gather up your personal belongings and, if you are so inclined, to attend her ladyship's funeral."

I watched in trepidation as the muscles in Violet's neck tightened in anger. Steady on, old girl, I thought to myself. Knowing my old friend as I do, I knew that tongue of hers could lash out with all the force of a mid-Atlantic gale.

"You're very kind, I'm sure, Lady Margaret," was the controlled response.

I breathed a sigh of relief. Still, like distant rumblings of thunder, there was a feeling of tension building within the room. I decided to stave off the approaching storm clouds by turning my attention to Sir Charles who, having returned to our little enclave, stood swirling the remaining contents of brandy around in his glass while absentmindedly humming a little melody to himself. A sharp glance from his wife abruptly terminated the tune.

"Please accept my condolences on the passing of your mother," I said.

"What? Oh, yes," he replied, a little startled, my words obviously breaking some train of thought. "Thank you, Mrs. Hudson. We shall all miss her terribly, I'm afraid."

"And the cause, if I may be so bold as to ask?"

"What?"

"The cause. The cause of death," I repeated, feeling three pairs of eyes boring into me. Still, I was interested in seeing what response my question would elicit from the St. Clairs.

"Ah, yes, the cause." Casting a sideways glance at his wife, I was once more subjected to a series of nervous coughs by the baronet.

"Our family physician attributes it to nothing more than a failure of the heart," interjected Lady Margaret, stepping in to take control of the uneasiness that prevailed within the room. "Unpleasant though it may be, Mrs. Hudson," she continued, in a condescending tone, "we must all face up to the fact that no one lives forever. After all, her ladyship was a woman well advanced in her years."

"Not that flamin' advanced, she weren't!" was my old friend's caustic comment.

Her remark had the effect of a bomb going off. While Sir Charles merely stood there fidgeting and looking uncomfortable, his wife turned absolutely livid. Gone was her sense of social decorum as her voice rose to a fever pitch.

"There are some people, Mrs. Hudson," although the eyes of Lady Margaret burned deep into Vi's, the words she spewed out were addressed to me, "who believe more in their active imaginations than they do in a doctor's report!"

I was staggered by this sudden outburst. It

would seem that beneath the ice queen's frosty exterior lay a smoldering temper. At that point, I thought it best we take our leave.

"Perhaps, Vi," I said, "we should . . ."

"Aye, right you are," she responded, pushing her hands against the arms of the chair and rising to a standing position. "We best be retiring for the night. You've eaten, have you, luv?"

"Yes, actually. I found myself a little tea shop in the village."

"Right, then. No need for you to be botherin' the servants, Sir Charles—I'll see to Mrs. Hudson's luggage."

I mentioned to Vi there was only a small valise as I had no idea of my length of stay. "You'll excuse us, then, Lady Margaret?" I said.

No answer was forthcoming.

"Sir Charles?"

"Yes, well, goodnight to you, Mrs. Hudson—Mrs. Warner," he replied, setting down his glass on the tea cart without looking at either one of us.

Once out in the foyer, Violet was kind enough to retrieve my valise from where it had been previously placed. I paused at the base of the staircase and, resting my hand on the dark walnut banister and gazing upward, it appeared to me to be as formidable a climb for someone of my years, as the Spanish Steps of Rome.

Violet noted my hesitancy as I took a deep breath before attempting to ascend.

" 'Ere," she announced with a chuckle, "it's not as bad as it looks."

And so saying, placed her arm under mine. "Wait," I said. "Listen."

In our haste to leave the study, I had left the door slightly ajar. We stood in silence on the bottom step listening to the St. Clairs' somewhat inaudible but highly spirited conversation—or at least, high spirited on the part of Lady Margaret.

"Wait here," I told Vi, tiptoeing back to the study.

"What's this, now! Eavesdroppin', is it? Oh, I shouldn't if I were you."

Despite her protestations, Violet quickly and quietly followed. Together, we pressed ourselves against the door and listened.

"And another thing, Charles, you speak to these people as if they were our equals!"

We watched in silence as his wife paced back and forth, passing from our vision at various intervals. I had a mind to ease the door open an extra inch but thought the better of it.

"It's bad enough," she continued, "that we have to endure that Warner woman at the dinner table each evening, now I suppose we'll have to set an extra chair for this Hodgeson person, or whatever her name is."

"What!" exclaimed Violet. "*She* has to endure *me*! Well, I like that!"

I pressed a finger to my lips in the hope of stilling her to silence as I watched Sir Charles very calmly accepting his wife's temperamental outburst with an air of amusement.

"Hudson, actually." He smiled.

"What?"

"Hudson," he answered, walking over to the bar. "The woman's name is Hudson. As for Mrs. Warner," he added, pausing to refill his glass before continuing, "you know very well, Margaret, it was Mother's wish that we treat her as one of the family."

He quickly downed his drink as if to fortify himself for the next onslaught. It wasn't long in coming.

"But your mother isn't with us anymore, is she?" She spat the words out at him. "And now we have this—Hudson woman with us. Who knows who will be knocking at our door tomorrow?"

The baronet, who had now moved into our line of vision, stood facing his wife.

"Really, Margaret," he replied in a soothing tone, "there's no need to get yourself in a dither. After all, they'll be gone by the end of the week. As I recall, you made that perfectly clear to the both of them."

"And a jolly good thing I did, too!" she exclaimed angrily. "What exactly is this Mrs. Hudson doing here anyway? I don't like it, Charles. You remember seeing the fuss Mrs. Warner made when she found your Mother had—had . . ."

"Passed away?"

She seized on his words. "Yes, that's it, passed away."

"Passed away, me flippin' foot!" exclaimed my companion, with an angry jab of her elbow in my side.

"And now," continued the lady of the manor, "this woman from London arrives on our doorstep. Why?"

"Steady on, old darling. You make it sound as if she's working undercover for Scotland Yard."

She whirled round to face him. "Why do you mention Scotland Yard?"

"I was under the impression," he replied in an offhanded manner, "it was where your line of thought was taking you."

"No, why should it?" She appeared quite agitated and for the first time since taking our stance outside the door, Lady Margaret's voice dropped to a slight whisper as she slumped into a chair, thereby partially obstructing our view of her. "Charles, we simply must sit down and rationally discuss what actually took place in your mother's bedroom."

At that remark, I again received another jab in the ribs.

"If you really think it's necessary, old darling. But not tonight, I'm afraid. You look tired. Why not trundle off to bed? Besides, we do have Mother's funeral to attend tomorrow. I say . . . !"

"What is it? What's the matter?"

"The door to the study. It hasn't been properly shut."

"It was probably that Hudson woman who left it ajar," she replied, with annoyance. "You'd best shut it, Charles."

It was now time to beat a hasty retreat. No longer did the staircase seem insurmountable. I ascended to the top as if on winged feet, with

Violet following close behind.

Down the hall we went and, on reaching the bedroom door, hurried inside with Vi, quickly locking it from within.

FIVE

Partners in Crime

AFTER HAVING RUN like a pair of errant schoolgirls up the stairs to the safety of the bedroom, we allowed ourselves time to regain our composure before Vi was good enough to give me a hand in putting away what little apparel I had brought with me.

"There's not much here, is there?" she asked, hanging up my navy blue dress with the ruffled lace neck in the closet.

"Originally, I had planned for no more than an overnight stay," I responded. "Now, it appears to be somewhat extended."

"Aye, but only 'til end of week, same as me. Well, I mean, you heard what Lady Uppity-Up said. Can you imagine—*her* giving *me* permission to attend the ruddy funeral! Now, I ask you! Aside from old Hogarth—"

"Hogarth?"

"Aye. The butler. As I was saying, it's me what's been the only one who ever cared for the old girl."

She crossed the room, over to a large ornate dresser. "You wouldn't care for a little nip to wet your whistle, would you, luv?" she asked, sliding open the second drawer down from the top.

"Why, Violet Warner!" I exclaimed in mock horror. "Don't tell me you've taken to hiding bottles in your bedroom!"

"Strictly for medicinal purposes only, you understand," she replied with a saucy wink, revealing a bottle of sherry.

As my companion set about the task of pouring the drinks, I settled myself down onto a slightly worn blue velvet settee, opposite a bed of indeterminate age and comfort. On the far wall a photograph of Violet and Albert stared back at me from above the mantelpiece.

"I remember the day you and Albert had that photo taken," I announced with a smile.

She gazed wistfully at the picture for a few moments before replying it was all she had kept from the old days.

"Unlike me," I replied with a chuckle. "I can never bring myself to throw anything away. Make no mistake, m'girl, someone will have a fine old time sorting it all out, after I'm gone."

After handing me my drink she fetched a cane-back chair from the corner and settled herself down opposite me.

"You know, Vi," I said, leaning forward, "when you first told me your mistress had been murdered, well, quite frankly, I thought that—" I was stumbling for just the right words.

"That I'd gone bonkers, right?"

Violet always had a way of coming right to the point.

I squirmed uneasily. "It would appear," I said, addressing the subject from another tack, "that the conversation we overheard in the study corroborates your story up to a point. That is to say, something strange, or at least out of the ordinary, occurred in her ladyship's bedchamber on the night in question."

"Oh, yes, I'd say murder was summat out of the ordinary, I would," she stated before taking a rather large swallow of her sherry. "And your Mr. Holmes," she queried, now eyeing the remaining contents of her drink, "when was it you said he'd be back?"

Her question was asked almost too casually, and while on the surface it seemed innocent enough, I could see she had been hurt by what she perceived as a lack of belief on my part and was anxious to have the renowned Sherlock Holmes take on the case.

"My dear Violet," I replied wearily, "neither Mr. Holmes nor for that matter Dr. Watson will be back from Scotland for at least a fortnight. By which time the trail will be cold, the clues nonexistent. Therefore, having taken the matter under deep consideration,"—this was a small white lie, for, in truth, I had only decided at that moment on my course of action— "I have resolved to take it upon myself to enter into my own investigation of the murder at Haddley Hall. The murder at Haddley Hall," I repeated with a smile. It sounded like a title Dr. Watson would have used.

"Right you are, then!" she sang out, taking my renewal of faith in her as good an opportunity as any to replenish her drink.

"But 'ere, now," she added, with a quizzical eye, "what's all this about you solvin' the murder, eh? You're no flamin' detective, least-ways, far as I know, you're not."

My response was immediate. "My dear Violet, I haven't lived with Sherlock Holmes all these years not to—" I stopped, a trifle embarrassed by the unintentional implication. "I mean," I continued, this time choosing my words more carefully, "the fact that Mr. Holmes has resided for many years as a paid lodger within my premises has afforded me the opportunity of observing investigative procedures at close hand. And," I added, lowering my voice, the better to heighten the confidentiality of the moment, "I have, on occasion, played no small part in various criminal cases the gentleman has undertaken."

"Wot's this, you're sayin'—that it's been you and Mr. Holmes wot's been solvin' all those crimes?"

"Not at all," I replied, drawing myself up. "Only that at one time or another I did make certain suggestions. Suggestions, I might add, my dear Mrs. Warner, that proved helpful in more than one circumstance."

"Strange, though, ain't it, like," was her puzzled and derisive reply, "that I never read about these here what you call 'suggestions' in any of the cases the doctor's written about."

"No—and you never shall! Pompous old fool!" I blurted out, giving vent to the frustration I had kept locked inside for too many years.

"Well, thank you very much, I'm sure!" At that, my companion made a move to rise from the chair.

"No, no, not you, Vi," I quickly responded. "I didn't mean you. I was speaking of Dr. Watson."

As she settled back, I placed my hand on hers in reassurance and openly confided that I had always felt it most unkind of the good doctor to have relegated me to a few inconsequential lines at best, without ever once setting down on paper the help I'd given over the years, however small or unimportant he may have felt it to have been. "Or for that matter," I continued, in the same irritable vein, "did he ever ask my permission to use my name? You'd think, from reading his stories, that I did nothing but serve meals or inform them when they had a caller."

I'm afraid Vi was quite taken aback by my candor. "Dr. Watson? Why, he seems like a right proper gent, he does. Leastways, what I've read about him."

"Make no mistake, m'girl," I responded. "Dr. John Watson is, by all accounts, the epitome of the proper Victorian gentleman. And, as such, he believes women, like small children and household pets, are best seen and not heard. Such are the times we live in."

"True enough, I suppose," was Violet's wistful reply. "But then, it's always been like that. Still, Dr. Watson—I mean . . ."

She was hedging on her words—and her thoughts.

"Oh, I know what you're thinking. Yes, perhaps I am being nothing but a vain, silly old woman." I paused, deciding not to pass on a silent offer of another drink. "And I suppose, to give the doctor his due," I continued, whilst holding my glass out before me, "I should mention he has been most helpful, medically speaking, on more than one occasion."

"Been ailin' then, have you luv?"

"Oh, just the usual aches and pains one acquires at our age."

My old friend nodded knowingly in silent reflection of various ailments past and present.

"Nevertheless," I announced with a spirited slap of hand to knee, "they haven't closed the lid down on me yet. And if there's a murder to be solved here, then, solve it I shall!"

At that point, I rose to my feet and quite melodramatically—could I be feeling the effects of the sherry—intoned, "Therefore, my dear, Violet Elizabeth Warner, I will, in effect, be *your* Sherlock Holmes!"

I received a puzzled look and then a widening smile. "And I'll be *your* Dr. Watson!" was Violet's triumphant response as she rose from her chair to join me in a standing position.

I moaned inwardly while somehow managing a semblance of a smile in return. I had no wish to be encumbered by any second party, being of a mind that the investigation would best be served if it were of a solitary nature. Still, since Violet was acquainted with those residing at the estate as well as the circumstances of the murder itself, she would certainly prove invaluable to me.

"Done!" I exclaimed.

The clinking of two sherry glasses formalized the new partnership.

SIX

—

An Out-of-Body Experience

&∞—LIKE A DYING body emitting a few last pitiful gasps and sighs, the charred log that lay upon the grate issued forth an occasional crackle and hiss until there remained, for one brief instant, a single spark of flame. Then, it too was gone. As if on cue, the wind, howling in wild lament outside the bedroom window, took this opportunity to make its chilling presence felt throughout the room.

I snuggled down deeper under the counterpane.

"Now Vi," I said, turning toward my companion, who lay next to me, "don't you dare fall asleep before telling me everything you know of Lady St. Clair's murder."

"Can't it wait 'til morning, then?" was the sleepy response.

"Until morning! I should say not! Do you think I could rest before hearing the tale told?" I gave her shoulder a nudge. "Vi, please!"

Grudgingly, she sat up in bed and I followed suit.

42

"I suppose," she said, pulling the counter-pane up around the both of us, "it would be best if I start at the beginning, like, other-wise—"

"You can start wherever you please! Only do get on with it." Whether it was due to the lateness of the hour, I don't know. But I was beginning to grow impatient with her.

"Well, I like that, I do!"

"I'm sorry, Vi," I replied, hoping to mollify her. "Please, tell it in your own way."

"Well, now, that's what I were trying to do, weren't it?" announced Violet in a manner my late husband always called Vi's "sweet and sour response." The smile was sweet, but the words were sour. I said no more as my com-panion turned her eyes from mine and seemed to be lost within her own private thoughts.

At last there came a clearing of her throat, which always signified, at least to Violet, that what she was about to say was of some con-siderable import. She began speaking rather softly. " 'Course, it means I'll have to tell you about . . ."

The rest of the words were mumbled.

"I'm sorry, dear. I didn't hear you." I shifted my position in bed toward her. "You were saying, you'll have to tell me about . . . ?"

"Me gift."

To make sure I had heard correctly, I re-peated the word. "Gift?"

"Aye. Me gift, as they calls it. Promise you won't laugh or anything like that."

My response was to give her hand a reas-suring squeeze.

"Right, then."

After readjusting herself to a more comfortable position, she began her story.

"You remember, don't you luv, the times we'd climb the stairs to old Bessie's flat to have our fortunes read?"

"Bessie—Bessie Muldoon." I said the name aloud more to myself than Vi and, in so doing, the gate of time opened, flooding my memory with a series of vignettes from days long past. As a widow her only source of income lay in the telling of fortunes, whether in the turn of a card or by the formation of leaves left at the bottom of an empty cup.

Looking back on it, it all seems rather silly now. But the time spent with Bessie did afford us an evening out by ourselves. Both William and Albert would, of course, have nothing to do with it and subjected the two of us to a great deal of good-natured teasing. But being men of the sea (a most superstitious lot) they never failed to inquire as to what the old lady had revealed. Which, I'm afraid, was nothing more than a generalization of what might or might not take place within any given period of time.

"Aye, that's right, Bessie Muldoon," nodded Vi in affirmation of my remembrance. "She were a good old soul, our Bessie was," she added with a smile, pleased with herself in having piqued my interest. "After you moved, I made the odd visit on my own. Not often, as I say, but I would nip in on occasion just to see how the old girl were keepin', more than anything else, like."

She stopped for a moment and held a forefinger up in the air. The reason being, I suppose, was to shift her sails in another direction
of thought before setting off on another tack.
I waited, trying to control my exasperation
with her ramblings. What on earth all this had
to do with the death of Lady St. Clair, I hadn't
the foggiest, and whether my old friend did or
not, remained to be seen. However, I hid my
annoyance as best I could while waiting for
her to continue.

"No, that's not true," she said at last. "The
thing of it was, I was becoming more involved,
you might say, with all that psychic folderol.
In fact, Bessie told me herself, on more than
one occasion, I had the gift meself."

"And just what is this gift of yours?"

"That's what they call it, luv, when you
have psychic powers. You see, it were like this.
One evenin' Bessie and I were having a nice
cup of tea upstairs in her sitting room, this being no more than a month before she passed
away, poor old thing, when I told her summat
I've never told a living soul before."

"Oh, yes, and what was that?"

"Well, there I was, lyin' in me bed one night
not really asleep and not really awake, if you
knows what I mean, when I gets this odd sensation of floatin' upwards. Like I say, I was
still in bed, mind you. I knew that, 'cause
when I looked down—there I were!"

"There you were?"

"Yes! Still lyin' in me bed! But me spirit
body or whatever, were floatin' up by the ceil-

ing, lookin' down at me! Well, you can imagine, I was ever so scared."

"Many's the nightmare I've had myself," said I.

"Nightmare!" she exclaimed. " 'Ere, t'weren't no ruddy nightmare. It really happened!"

I started to speak but lost the opportunity. There was no stopping Vi once she was under full sail.

"And that's only the half of it," she continued, in much the same animated fashion. "How can I be in two places at the same time, I asks meself. It ain't natural, like. And then I thinks, this is it, old girl, you're dead, you are. But I couldn't be in heaven or the other place 'cause I were still in me bedroom! It was all very confusin'. But I just knew, don't ask me how, that if I could get back into me body everythin' would be all right. And with that thought in mind, quicker than you can say, 'Bob's your uncle,' I was back in bed. Now, what do you think of that?"

"Extraordinary!" I exclaimed, it being the first applicable as well as noncommittal word that sprang immediately to mind.

"Aye, it were that all right. Well, now, I couldn't keep summat like that to meself for very long, now could I? Since my Bert had passed away, the only one I could turn to was Bessie. She didn't seem in the least surprised. Said I had had an O.B.E. Here, I says, what's that mean—Order of the British Empire? I thought the old girl had gone flamin' bonkers. 'No, dearie,' she says, smilin' that big toothless grin of hers, 'an out-of-body experience, that's what you've had m'girl.' "

"Of course!" I responded, excitedly. "Astral projection!"

"Aye, that's right, astral projection. Know all about it now, I do, thanks to Bessie. Explained it all to me, she did. But, 'ere," she queried, "how did you know?"

"My dear Violet," I announced in a rather haughty tone, "do give me some credit for being knowledgeable in areas outside the mainstream of social life."

Actually, my affectation of being a woman well versed in the subject of the occult was somewhat a pose on my part. In truth, only a few short months previously I had brought home a book on psychic phenomena, and for some strange reason, I found the chapter dealing with astral projection quite fascinating. So much so that I broached Mr. Holmes on that very matter.

His response, as I recall all too well, had been to airily dismiss the entire subject as being nothing more than a subconscious wish within the human mind to prove the existence of a spiritual self. It was his belief that the so-called parting of soul from body was nothing more than a flight of fancy on the part of the believer. He dealt, he assured me, in fact. And, since no hard scientific evidence pertaining to the supernatural existed, the whole discussion was, from his point of view, academic at best. I, on the other hand, took a less clinical and more humanistic approach to the subject.

"In essence, what you are telling me, Vi," I

said, propping up a pillow behind my back, "is that, whilst in a state of deep meditation, your spirit was able to release itself from the confines of your physical self, and in so doing, you were in a position to observe your earthly body as easily as you would your reflected image in a mirror."

"Aye!" she gasped. "That's it, exactly!"

"And being in such a state," I went on, "it is possible for the spiritual self to actually pass through the very walls themselves, and indeed, to float off to great distances."

"Then you do believe me!" Vi cried out, clapping her hands in delight at having found a spiritual cohort.

"Well," I hedged, "let's just say I keep an open mind on the subject." The result of my somewhat ambiguous reply was a sharp retort from my companion.

"An open mind, she says! Oh, yes, I can see you've got an open mind, all right! Well, let me tell you summat, Emma Hudson," she continued, in the same irritable manner, "I've passed through many a door and wall in my time, I have!"

I was taken totally by surprise. "What are you saying, Violet? You don't mean you've actually . . ."

I was the recipient of a smug, self-satisfied smile.

"That's right," she said. "I practiced, I did. Just like old Bessie told me. I mean, what else has an old bird like me got to do of an evenin', eh? It were, well, like a pastime, you might say. 'Course, I never flitted off very far, mind you. Sometimes no farther than the end of Porter Street and back." She sat there, arms folded defensively, before adding, "And it makes no never mind to me whether you believe me or not!"

Good Lord, I thought, what would Mr. Holmes's reaction have been to such an admission of astral adventure? I'll wager Vi would have received no more than a quick handshake and a thank you very much from a bemused and cynical Mr. H before that gentleman extricated himself from what he would most assuredly have described as a tale told by a madwoman. How fortunate for my companion it was I and not Sherlock Holmes in whom she had confided.

"Violet, Violet, Violet," I repeated, cupping my hands round hers, "I believe you, I truly do. You've always been a strange one, m'girl, but I've never known you to lie."

A tear appeared, and making its watery descent down her cheek, rested on a trembling lip.

"Oh, Em," she sobbed, "it's that glad I am you're here."

As if on some prearranged signal, we turned and flung our arms around each other in a warm and quietly comforting embrace. And though inwardly in an emotional state myself, I broke the silence by addressing my old friend in a cool and collected manner.

"Now, then, Mrs. Warner, let's have it—the rest of the story, if you please."

"Right, then," she replied, dabbing her eyes and bringing herself back once more into a sitting position. And, as she did so, I quickly and unobtrusively brushed a tear aside myself. Violet cleared her throat. She was ready to tell the tale.

"It all began Saturday night," she announced. "I was lyin' in this very bed. 'Course, at that time, I didn't know it was going to be the night of the murder, 'til later like, you understand."

"Yes, yes. Go on," I prodded.

"Well, I'm all snuggled down and cozy, like, when I remembered I'd forgotten to look in on her ladyship before retiring, being as how I always made it a point to pop in just to see if she were all right. So, like I says, I'm lyin' there, nice and warm, and feelin' that tired, when it occurs to me that maybe it wouldn't do any harm if I was to just sorta 'float in,' if you know what I mean. Otherwise, it meant getting out of bed, putting on me housecoat, and traipsin' off down the hall. Well, I ask you, can you blame me?"

"In other words," was my straight-faced comment, "the spirit was willing, but the flesh was weak."

That garnered a chuckle from Vi.

"Oh, I like that, I do. Spirit was willin'—" Again a chuckle. "You surprise me, you do, Em."

"Really, Violet," I replied, not knowing whether to feel hurt or not. "I am not entirely without a sense of humor."

"Oh, yes, you'd have 'em rollin' in the aisles at the Gaiety, you would."

"Vi, please!"

"Right," she said, stifling a smile. "Now where was I? Oh, yes. So, I ups and glides down the hall to her ladyship's bedroom."

"Just like that?"

"Aye. It don't take me long to float off once I sets me mind to it."

Although I still found it difficult to believe in what I was hearing, I could think of no apparent reason why it should not be so. Straight as an arrow, this Manchester lass. However, there was certain data I hoped to glean from her story.

"Just where is her ladyship's bedroom in relationship to yours?"

"Three doors down. But the hallway at night is colder than an Eskimo's nose. That were another advantage to go floatin' off. When I'm in me spirit body, I feels neither cold nor warm. Strange, like, ain't it?"

She carried on, not waiting for my reply. Her question being rhetorical, in any event.

"So, there's me in her bedroom and it bein' blacker than a chimneysweep's ear. If it hadn't been for a sliver of moonlight slippin' in through the half-closed drapes, I'd never 'ave seen him."

"Seen him? Seen who?"

"Well, that's just it, isn't it—I don't know! He were just a dark shape to me, bending over her ladyship, like he was. But from what I could make out, he had a white cloth or summat over the old girl's face."

I must confess her story filled me with horror as well as a tinge of excitement. "What happened next?" I blurted out.

"Screamed bloody murder, I did. And when I sees her flingin' her arms about and strugglin' to get free, I flung myself at him. Fat lot of good that did. I'd forgot, you see, when I'm in me spirit form, I can't be seen, heard, or felt. Passed right through, I did—like a ruddy ghost!"

"You speak of this person as if it were a man. Can you be sure about that?"

"Well, I don't know. I just assumed, like."

"Ah, but my dear Violet," I replied professorially, as befitted my newfound role as private investigator, "one must never assume anything. An assumption is completely without foundation, relying as it does on intuition at best. Facts, m'girl, are what we need. Facts."

"At the time it weren't flamin' facts I was interested in!" was the angry rejoinder. "All I knew were that I couldn't be of any help to her ladyship floatin' around the room like a bloomin' butterfly! So, I wills meself back. And," she continued, placing her hand on mine, "don't ask me where I got me nerve from, Em, but as soon's I'm back in me body, I throws on me housecoat and goes chargin' down the hall to the old girl's bedroom."

"Vi!" I gasped. "That could have been extremely dangerous. You informed no one?"

"Oh, aye. The whole ruddy household, screamin' like I did and bangin' on the door. Here, I shouts, I know you're in there!"

"The door was locked, then?"

"Aye. That made me all the more upset as her ladyship made it a rule never to have it locked. 'Fraid of fire, you see. Didn't want to be messin' about tryin' to get it open. So, there I stands, bellowin' like a banshee, 'til old Hogarth comes along with candle and his ring of keys."

"Didn't it seem odd to you that he would appear on the scene when he did?" I asked.

"No, not really," was her unconcerned response. "The old boy always makes his rounds every night seeing to it everything is as it should be."

"Oh."

Deflated by her answer, I comforted myself with the thought that while his arrival may have been routine, I was right in raising the point. No stone left unturned, that sort of thing. I bade her continue.

"So, in we goes with Hogarth holdin' the candle above his head so's to spread the light that much farther and me expectin' any minute someone to be jumpin' out of the shadows. And when I looks all around, there he was, gone!"

"There he was—gone? Oh, Vi, really!"

"Well, you know what I mean." She fluttered her hands about in exasperation at my having dropped anchor on her, as it were, while under a full head of steam. Then, after I had received what Violet deemed to be a suitable look of annoyance, she continued.

"By this time, the whole ruddy family, having heard the racket I was raisin' in the hallway, comes runnin' into the room to see me by the bed and Hogarth holdin' the candle over the old lady's face. Then Lady Margaret strides over and, calmly as you please, announces, 'I'm afraid her ladyship is dead.' So the doctor elbows his way through to examine her. 'Yes,' he says, 'it appears her heart gave out on her. At least we can be thankful she passed away quietly.' 'Quietly!' I screams. Oh, I were that upset. 'I saw a bloke in here not one minute ago,' I says. 'He's the one who did her in. It weren't no flamin' heart attack!' 'The woman obviously has taken leave of her senses,' says Missy Prim-and-Proper. The squire turns to Hogarth and asks him what he knows about all this, and Hogarth—"

"One moment, Vi," said I. "Before you get too far into your story, I think it best if you acquaint me with those present within the room. It would give me a better understanding—"

"Oh, that's right, you don't know, do you, luv? Well, now, let's see. There were Sir Charles, of course, and Lady Margaret, you've met them. And then there were Dr. Morley, him bein' the family's personal physician, like, and the squire. That's Henry St. Clair, Sir Charles's brother. And who else, oh, yes, the colonel."

"The colonel?"

"Colonel Wyndgate, though I've heard the servants call him Colonel Windbag behind his back on more than one occasion, and rightly so, if you ask me. He were an old army friend of his lordship. Stays on here at Haddley, he does."

"And this, Henry St. Clair, the squire, what do you know about him?"

"He'd be a year or two younger than Sir

Charles. Runs the estate, though you'd never know it. Spends most of his time in London at the gaming tables. As does Sir Charles. Not at the tables, mind you, but in London. Sits on the board as chairman for some big banking firm. I don't know which one. They never tells me much. And that's it."

"Except for Hogarth," I reminded her.

"Oh, yes, Hogarth. Well, it's easy enough to forget about him, ain't it? Sorta blends in with the furniture, you might say. Been around longer than Stonehenge, he has. I daresay he knows more about the family than anyone."

I made a mental note of the information and reminded myself to put it down on paper on the morrow.

"Well, do go on, Vi." Seeing she was becoming somewhat weary, I gave her arm a little nudge. "You were telling me about the squire asking Hogarth . . . ?"

"Aye, that's right," she said, smothering a yawn. "Hogarth tells him, right enough, that when he saw me banging on her ladyship's door, he undid the lock, and followed me in. 'Did you see anyone else in the room other than Lady St. Clair?' the squire asks him. 'No, sir,' he answers. Then Sir Charles speaks up. 'Why on earth, Mrs. Warner,' he asks me, 'did you say you *saw* someone in the room when it's quite obvious from what Hogarth has told us, you were *outside* the door when he arrived on the scene?'

"Well, he had me there, didn't he? I mean, I couldn't tell them about—you know what. They'd 'ave had me bundled off to Bedlam without so much as a by-your-leave. So, thinkin' fast like, I says, I just had a feelin' that's all. Call it woman's intuition, if you like. That didn't set too well with Lady Big-wig. 'Mrs. Warner,' she says, in that snippy way of hers, 'it would appear you've either had a bad dream or else your mental capacities are deteriorating with age. In either case, it would be best if you left us now.' "

"What did you say to that?"

"Nothing. I ignored her, as usual. And bein' that upset, as I was, with the passin' of me mistress, and all, I bent down to give her ladyship one last kiss on the cheek. Now, me nose ain't all that good. Can't smell things the way I used to. But, oh, when I leaned over her, I did smell summat right funny, like. Here, I says, that's a queer smell for you! Well, they all gathered round and not a one of them would admit they smelled anythin'. Not a one of them!"

"Most puzzling. Not even the doctor?"

" 'It's a musty old room, Mrs. Warner. It could be anything,' was the best I could get out of him."

"And Hogarth?"

"He'd left by then. I believe Sir Charles had asked him to see about sending one of the help for an undertaker, first thing in the morning."

"What was the odor, do you suppose?" I asked. Although at that point, I had my own suspicions. But if Vi had any way of confirming them, so much the better.

"It weren't 'til next mornin' when it strikes me where I had smelled it once before. It were the time my Bert were in hospital. Chlory-form, it was. Well, I mean, I didn't know what to do, did I? Then I thought of you and Mr. Holmes. That's when I decided to send the telegram."

"Chloroform—I thought as much!" I admit I rubbed my hands in glee. A cloth soaked in chloroform and pressed over the old woman's face was all that was needed to do the deed. I was beginning to understand why both Mr. Holmes and Dr. Watson found criminal inves-tigation to be such a fascinating adventure.

Violet had given me much to ponder. I thought it best to review what I had learned before giving in to a much-needed sleep. There could now be no doubt that someone had in-deed entered Lady St. Clair's bedchamber and taken the old woman's life. But why did not one among those present, save for Vi, admit to being aware of the odor of a vaporous chemical within the room? And if Violet could smell it, the odor must have been quite pun-gent, indeed. Baffling. Most baffling. As to the scene of the crime, it would not have been pos-sible for the murderer to make good an escape without being seen in the corridor by either Vi or Hogarth, given how so little time had elapsed. To follow that line of thought, the murderer should still have been present within the room when Violet and the butler entered. Then how—? A secret panel? Per-haps. Questions within questions. None of which, I told myself, were going to be an-swered that night.

I was now at a point of welcoming sleep as I would an old friend. I glanced over at Vi and was not surprised to find her already deep in slumber, mouth agape and, though she would never have admitted it, snoring lightly at irregular intervals. I blew out the candle, slid down under the covers, and quietly drifted off.

With the clock on the mantel not being visible to me within the darkened room, how long I remained asleep before being awakened by the sound of angry yet muffled voices, I had no idea. Vi was still asleep, her snoring told me that much, and I had no intention of wakening her.

I raised myself up on one elbow. There—again! Only now it was the sound of someone crying. A young woman, or a boy, perhaps. Where was it coming from? The anguished cries were too low for me to properly judge what particular area of the house they were coming from. The room above? Perhaps.

I remember feeling completely exhausted. The last sound of which I was aware before once more succumbing to sleep was of a heavy thump, like that of a body falling to the floor.

SEVEN

A Deadly Arrival

᷾THE FOLLOWING MORNING, as Vi and I were descending the staircase, we were met by Hogarth achingly making his way up toward us.

"Mrs. Warner—Mrs. Hudson," he wheezed, resting his hand on the banister in an effort to catch his breath. "I was just on my way up to inform you that breakfast will be delayed until—"

"What!" Vi cut in. "Summat's happened to Cook, then? And me what was lookin' forward to a nice plate of kippers and bangers. Well, there you are, you see," said she, with a sigh, "even in a place as grand as this, you never know when your next meal will be turning up."

"There's nothing wrong with Cook, Mrs. Warner," Hogarth responded. "I'm afraid it's more serious than that. The police are here."

"The police!" we cried out in unison.

"An inspector and a constable from Twillings, Mrs. Hudson."

I remembered Twillings as being the name of the village where I'd met the farmer who escorted me to the estate.

"What's this all about, Hogarth?" I asked.

Although visibly distressed, the old gentleman's years of servitude enabled him to maintain a certain sense of decorum appropriate to any occasion.

"Sir Charles," he stated, with only the slightest trace of a quiver to his voice, "has complied with the inspector's request that the family as well as those staying at the estate, save for the household staff, gather in the music room at their earliest convenience, madam."

"Not the household staff?"

"They, as well as I, have already been questioned, Mrs. Hudson."

"At last summat's bein' done!" exclaimed Violet. Then, eyeing Hogarth she added, " 'Ere, this *is* about her ladyship, ain't it?"

"I'm afraid, Mrs. Warner," was the old gentleman's guarded response, "that it would not be prudent on my part to volunteer more information than I have already."

"But, Hogarth," I began, then stopped as he averted his eyes from mine and bit his lip in bottled-up frustration.

I felt there was much he could tell us, but he remained ever the perfect butler. I pressed him no further, being left to wonder if someone had indeed spoken up about the demise of the late Lady St. Clair. And, if so—who? Violet, I surmised, had similar thoughts, for we exchanged puzzled glances as we descended the staircase and made our way to the music room.

"Yes, do come in, ladies," spoke Sir Charles as we hesitated momentarily outside the open door. "That about completes the circle, as it were," he added, addressing a smallish man with a bushy broom moustache, standing just to our left, wearing a topcoat with a black bowler clamped tightly to his head. Strange, I thought. Were they so intimidated by the gentleman's presence as to forego a request for the removal of his hat?

I looked about the room to see Lady Margaret, solemnly attired in black brocade standing by her husband, to the left of the piano.

Good Lord, I wondered, what time in the morning does that woman get up to make herself look so presentable?

Aside from the St. Clairs and the man, who evidently was the inspector of whom Hogarth had spoke, there were three other gentlemen present. Two were standing, talking quietly together, and the third had taken a position beside the window. Any appraisal I could have made of all three was abruptly curtailed by a voice asking, "And you are—?"

It was Broom Moustache.

"Mrs. Hudson," I replied, introducing myself. "And this is Mrs. Warner, an old friend and former lady's companion to the late Lady St. Clair, Inspector . . . ?"

"Thackeray, madam. Inspector Jonas Thackeray, of the Twillings constabulary. Now, then, ladies," he began in a dry monotone, "as I have already informed those present—"

He was cut off in mid-sentence by Vi inter-jecting an apology on behalf of our tardiness. "Excuse me, Inspector, we'd of been down earlier, but Em, Mrs. Hudson, that is, and I, were up half the night. Talkin' we were, 'til all hours. I'm usually awake . . ."

She was stopped by an eyebrow that slowly arched itself up toward the rim of the bowler while beady eyes glowered at her from be-neath the brim.

"If you please, madam!"

As Vi and I took the opportunity of seating ourselves on two rather large uncomfortable chairs, I noticed the two men who had been talking together earlier had taken their place on the sofa.

"I shall begin again . . ."

"Inspector Thackeray!" Lady Margaret's voice sliced the air. "If you feel something is about to fall on your head, by all means keep your hat on, otherwise—"

The poor inspector, looking as embarrassed as a small boy at a ladies' tea, pulled the of-fending bowler from his head and placed it on the table.

Good for you, Lady Margaret, thought I.

"You'll have to excuse me, m'lady," he stammered. "I don't realize I have it on half the time. In fact," he continued, in an obvious attempt to cover up his embarrassment, "my missus says I'd wear it to bed if she didn't . . ."

There was a shuffling of feet. Sir Charles coughed.

In an attempt to regain his composure, the

inspector hastily withdrew a small note pad and pencil from the inside pocket of his top-coat.

"Yes, well, I'll begin again then, shall I?"

A slight pause on the inspector's part while his questioning eyes surveyed the room. Satisfied he would be able to proceed without further interruption, he plunged right in. "The body of a young woman," he began, "whose identity for the moment remains unknown, was found on the grounds of the estate in the early hours of the morning by . . ."—he paused for a quick scan of his notes—"a Will Tadlock, employed at Haddley as groom's helper. Cause of death due to the head being forcibly struck from behind by some type of heavy, blunt instrument. A preliminary examination of the body by Dr. Morley," he continued, "puts the time of the murder somewhere between eleven o'clock last night and one o'clock this morning."

"Murdered! A young woman!" I cupped my hand to my mouth to stifle a gasp. Feeling I was about to faint, I leaned over to Vi's chair and grasped her arm for support. She remained rooted in her chair, her initial response of open-mouthed astonishment at last giving way to a cry of despair.

"Not Mary!"

Thackeray whirled on her. "Mary? Mary, who?"

"Mary O'Connell, Inspector, the under-house parlor maid," spoke the man by the window who, I presumed from his features—prominent nose and same weak chinline—

would be Squire St. Clair, younger brother to Sir Charles.

"No, Mrs. Warner, it wasn't Mary," he assured her. "There was a viewing of the body earlier this morning and I can assure you it was not the O'Connell girl."

"Well, thanks be for that," was my companion's relieved response. "But 'ere," she questioned the inspector, "just who is it out there, eh?"

The answer was given with no small annoyance. "That, Mrs. Warner, is what I'm trying to find out!"

"Inspector Thackeray," I spoke up, "are you telling us a woman has been brutally murdered, here on the premises, and yet no one knows just who the poor creature is? You've questioned everyone, I take it?"

"Yes, Mrs. Hudson," was the tight-lipped reply. "Everyone—except you and Mrs. Warner."

Fortunately, at this point, Hogarth entered, postponing for the moment anything further from the good inspector.

"Tea, as requested, m'lady."

"Thank you, Hogarth. Over there would be fine," Lady Margaret said, indicating with a turn of her head a table of the Queen Anne period placed to the center of an open-draped bay window.

As the old gentleman proceeded across the room, October's early morning sunlight streamed through the window with rays brilliantly bouncing off the circular silver tray and tea service set around an arrangement of light pastry.

"Ah, Margaret to the rescue!" was Sir Charles's bemused response to the offering.

"I know you would have preferred something stronger, Charles, even at this early hour of the morning. But do try to bear up—at least until noon."

"I say, old darling, you'll have Thackeray here thinking I'm the family sot. Not true, sir, I assure you. Still, I see nothing wrong with a whiskey or two helping one to escape the realities of the world. Far more enjoyable than an evening at cards—and less expensive, too. Wouldn't you agree, Henry?"

The squire brushed aside the remark with a hollow laugh.

I turned my attention to the old butler silently taking his leave. On reaching the door, he paused momentarily before turning back to face me. Although not a word was exchanged by either party, those sad and tired eyes spoke volumes.

Hogarth, thought I, after fetching Vi and myself some tea and returning to my seat, at a more opportune time, you and I are going to have ourselves a nice little chat. A few moments later, I noticed that one of the three previously seated gentlemen had left his chair and was advancing toward me.

"Wyndgate, madam. Colonel Wyndgate. Royal North Surrey, retired," he stated by way of introduction.

A portly gentleman with a magnificent white walrus moustache that drooped to either

side of his chin (chins?) stood before me.
Flakes of crumbs from the pastry held in a
beefy hand fell upon a waistcoat whose but-
tons appeared to be engaged in a desperate
game of tug-o-war with an oversized stomach.

"Colonel," I replied, in acknowledgment of
his introduction, however blunt.

"Hudson, is it?"

"*Mrs.* Hudson, yes."

"Hudson," he repeated, with a vacant stare.
"Had a chap in my regiment named Hudson.
Never did like the fellow. Not your husband,
I suppose."

"My husband," I coldly replied, "served at
sea."

"Sea, you say! Navy man then, was he?"

"Merchant," I stated sharply, for I was becoming a trifle annoyed.

"Oh, those fellows. Well, never mind, we all
do what we can."

"If you'll excuse me, Colonel," I said. "I
think I'm in need of a refill." I wasn't, but it
was one way of extricating myself from his
presence.

"Beastly business this, what?"

Was he hard of hearing or just ignoring my
attempt at a tactful withdrawal? I turned my
attention back to him. Although I doubted
whether this pompous bloat could tell me anything, it was an opportunity I could not pass
up.

"The young woman, you mean?"

"Yes, quite."

"You have no knowledge of her, yourself?"

He licked a spot of jam that had fallen onto

his fingers from the half-eaten pastry before replying, "Me? Good heavens, no, madam! Never saw the creature before in my life. Pretty enough young thing, though."

"You viewed the remains, then?"

"Indeed I did, madam. In fact, we all trooped out like soldiers on parade earlier this morning. All except Lady Margaret, of course. No need for her ladyship to see that sort of thing. Not proper, y'understand."

"Ah, yes," I responded, with a subtlety of sarcasm that would have done Violet proud, "the rules of social etiquette would, of course, override even an official investigation of a murder."

"Yes, that's it exactly," he answered, chomping into the last remains of his puff pastry.

The inspector, fearing his investigation was turning into little better than a tea social, tried to regain control of the situation.

"Please, ladies and gentlemen," he said, raising his voice. "I realize you have the funeral of her ladyship to attend today, so if you'll just bear with me, I shan't keep you any longer than necessary."

As the babble of voices ceased, Violet took the opportunity of replacing our empty cups on the tea cart and returned to her seat.

"Now, then, Mrs. Warner," spoke the inspector, turning his attention to Violet, "I believe the room you occupy overlooks the grounds to the rear of the estate where the body was found."

"Aye, that's right," Vi responded. "If that's where she was found."

"She was indeed, madam. Off the path leading up to the gazebo, actually. And, as you mentioned earlier that both you and Mrs. Hudson were up late last night, did either of you by any chance see or hear anything out of the ordinary?"

"How could we see anything? We were in bed, not standing by the ruddy window!"

"Nor hear anything, then?" His eyes darted back and forth between the two of us.

"Hear anything? Not me. 'Course, now, me hearing isn't as good as it once was. How about you, Em?"

"Hear anything?" I repeated.

At that moment the remembrance from the night before of muffled voices and anguished cries flashed through my mind. Yet the cries had come from within the house, of that I was sure. Or was I? Perhaps it was no more than an overactive imagination at work. Should I speak? If so, what then? I'd look like a foolish old woman. I wanted time to sort this out for myself.

"No, nothing," I replied.

"I see." The inspector sighed a weary sigh as pad and pencil were replaced in his pocket. Then, addressing the room, he asked, "May I assume no one has any knowledge, whatsoever, of the deceased?"

"It would seem, Inspector," stated Sir Charles, "that the young woman is a complete mystery to us all."

"Gypsy girl, if you ask me. Saw one of their

caravans only last week. Probably had a falling out with the clan and they dumped her here. Nasty beggars, the lot of 'em," was the colonel's contribution.

"We will, of course, be checking into that as well," Thackeray responded dryly.

"Good man, good man," puffed the old soldier.

"Well, thank you very much, ladies and gentlemen, you have been most helpful," said the inspector, with little or no conviction in his voice. "Although, I should point out further questioning may be necessary at a later date. I don't suppose," he added as an afterthought, "anyone will be going very far, in any event."

Violet spoke up. "Em, Mrs. Hudson, that is, and meself, were to leave by end of week. 'Course, now," she added, casting an eye toward the baronet's wife, "we could stay on a little longer, like. I'm sure her ladyship wouldn't mind. Would you, Lady Margaret?"

A crocodile smile would be the best way of describing the sly smirk that accompanied Violet's question.

Ignoring Violet, the woman in black brocade directed her response toward Thackeray. "Is it really necessary, Inspector?"

"If they were to stay on for at least a while longer, it would be more convenient all round," he replied, adding, "it is, after all, a murder investigation, m'lady."

There was a slight pursing of Lady Margaret's lips before that regal head gave way to an affirmative nod.

Violet turned to me with a trace of a smile

playing at the corners of her mouth. It was a triumph, of sorts, for our side, however small. Yet, if we had been denied additional time at Haddley, our investigation, for all intents and purposes, would have come to a dead end.

"Right, then," said the inspector. Then, taking note of a beckoning wave from the squire, he quickly excused himself from our presence.

As he left, my attention was drawn to a well-built man of ruddy complexion and salt and pepper hair which, I noted, was badly in need of a trim. Standing now, off to my side, quietly sipping his tea, in a suit slightly worn and crumpled, he gave the appearance of a man who had somehow wandered into this elegantly attired enclave by mistake. From where I sat, I took note that his face carried within it a certain sensitivity. Not, I thought, a strong-willed or forceful man, but nonetheless, a pleasant one. As if sensing he was the object of a silent appraisal, he turned and, meeting my gaze, nodded politely and approached.

Eyes of warm blue smiled down on me. "I don't believe we've been formally introduced," was the friendly opening. "I'm Dr. Morley. Dr. Thomas Morley."

"Oh," said Vi, stepping in, "I am sorry, Doctor. This," she replied, with a warm smile and a pat to my arm, "is my old friend from London, Mrs. Hudson."

"Good morning, Doctor," was my cordial response. "We meet under unfortunate circumstances, I'm afraid."

"Indeed we do, Mrs. Hudson. Especially

with the funeral and all. You will be going, I take it—to the funeral, that is."

"No," I responded. "I think not."

"Not going!" exclaimed my old companion. "Why ever not?"

"My dear Violet, I am not a member of the household nor did I know her ladyship. Besides," I added, "I am still a trifle weary from yesterday and an afternoon nap would not, I think, be amiss."

Not true. But I had no intention of revealing my plans for the afternoon to Vi in front of my new acquaintance.

"Oh," she responded in a childlike whine, "I am disappointed. Not going."

"Well, then," spoke the doctor, "we shall no doubt be seeing you later on."

"Dr. Morley. One moment, please," I said, on rising from my chair.

"Yes?"

"When you examined the body this morning," I asked, as if the question were no more than a casual afterthought, "did it appear to you a struggle had taken place?"

"No."

That was it. Nothing more. I had hoped he would have been more forthcoming but it seemed extracting information from him would be the equivalent of chipping away at a diamond. However, I was not to be put off so easily. "You found nothing to indicate . . . ?"

He stiffened slightly as that once engaging smile of his slowly disappeared into the corners of his mouth.

"What I found, Mrs. Hudson," he answered, in words balanced between affability and annoyance, "is what Inspector Thackeray has already told you. The young woman was killed by being struck on the head with a heavy, blunt instrument."

"No trace of chlory-form with this one, eh, Doctor?" remarked Vi, on rising to a standing position.

I screamed inwardly at my friend's indiscretion in disclosing to anyone what meager knowledge we had thus far obtained. I nervously awaited his reaction. Ah, there it was. An ever so slight raising of an eyebrow, or was it merely a twitch? Very much in control of himself, our Dr. Morley.

"Chloroform? I, ah, have no idea what you're talking about, Mrs. Warner."

"There were no other injuries to the young woman's body, Doctor, other than what you have already described?" I put the question to him in the hope it would erase from his mind, for the moment at least, Vi's reference to chloroform.

As I awaited my answer, those eyes, once a warm blue, dropped considerably in temperature. "Mrs. Hudson," he responded, deftly sidestepping my question, "I fail to see your interest in all this. Do you have some sort of medical background?"

How to answer that? It was Vi who came to my rescue.

" 'Ere now, Doctor," she responded with a light-hearted chuckle, "you know how we women are. A little bit of gossip wouldn't hurt

Em and me from being the center of attention at the next meeting of the ladies' sewing circle."

Good for you, Vi!

Although my old friend's on-the-spot fabrication put us in the position of being nothing more than two silly old biddies, it did garner a reply.

"The body," he answered, with eyes darting anxiously about the room as if seeking an avenue of escape from two silly old women, "will, of course, be examined more thoroughly by the local coroner at Twillings. I would suggest if you require more information, ladies, you'd best contact him. Now, if you'll excuse me."

"Well, Em," whispered Vi as the good doctor took his leave of us, "what do you think of him, eh?"

"Outwardly, quite personable, I should say. Until one steps in too close, then up goes a barrier as defensive as the great wall of China."

"Aye. Right enough, I suppose," replied Violet. "Still, doctors never do like having their judgment questioned, do they?"

I noted that the inspector, partially obscured by the potted palm at the entrance to the french doors, had ended his conversation with the squire and was about to take his leave.

"Vi," I said. "There's something I want to speak to the inspector about. It might be better if I went alone. Would you mind?" With her approval I made my way across the carpeted floor over to the inspector, feeling a little uneasy as to how I would be received.

"Inspector Thackeray."

"Yes, Mrs. Hudson?"

I took him by the arm and unobtrusively escorted him out the door, the better to speak to him in private.

"The body of the young woman—has it been removed as yet?"

"I was just on my way to see that it was. Why do you ask?"

"I should like to view the remains."

"A most macabre request, Mrs. Hudson, if I may say so," he answered, studying me most carefully before adding, "is there something you're not telling me?"

I now believed it would be more prudent on my part to seek official and professional assistance. Mr. Holmes had made use of the police in certain instances, and I believed the situation now warranted the inspector being made aware of the events as I saw them, at least, up to a point. However, since it was my first case, I decided it would be best to tread carefully.

"I'll explain more fully outside," I confided.

He eyed me somewhat warily for a moment or two before replying in measured tones, "Very well, Mrs. Hudson, come with me."

EIGHT

Grounds for Murder

⁐WE FOLLOWED A pebbled path that wound its way through the landscaped grounds and continued on down a series of stone steps set within the gently sloping hills until at last we came to level ground. Trees, bereft of all but a few last vestiges of their autumn foliage, afforded me a limited view of a small lake responding in agitated annoyance to an ever-increasing easterly wind. With the sun engaged in an atmospheric game of hide-and-seek with slate-gray clouds of ominous proportion I mentally congratulated myself on having thought to wear my shawl. With little warmth to be found within the halls of Haddley I had taken the precaution to put it on while dressing that morning. And, pulling it even tighter around me, I pictured myself here on a deliciously warm June day with straw hat, wide of brim, brushes and easel before me, happily transposing a myriad of color to canvas.

"It must be beautiful in the summer," I commented, looking over the now-bleak terrain.

"It was at one time," the inspector answered, turning his coat collar up before thrusting his hands deep into the pockets. "But it's not been kept up the way it once was. At least, that's what they tell me."

"They?"

"The locals, ma'am, from Twillings." He continued speaking without slowing his pace, and I was hard pressed to keep up with him. "There was a time when the old boy, or rather, I should say, his lordship, the earl of Haddley, made the grounds available to the townspeople one weekend every summer. Great tents were set up, musicians were hired to stroll the grounds, light refreshments were served. That sort of thing."

"You never went yourself?"

"Lord St. Clair had been dead for over three years when I arrived to take up my position. His wife, they say, would have liked to carry on the tradition. But *that* group," he added, indicating with a turn of his head toward the manor, "disbanded the practice on his lordship's death."

"The family isn't that well liked, I take it?"

"That's not for me to say, Mrs. Hudson."

And, in so saying, he had answered my question.

"From London, are you, Inspector?"

He eyed me quizzically.

"Your accent," I smiled.

"Oh. Yes. The missus, though, is from these parts. She never did like the grime and crime of the big city. Nor I, for that matter. When the opportunity presented itself at Twillings, we took our leave. And it's been peaceful enough, up until now, I'll say that much. The records show there hasn't been a murder reported here for over fifteen years."

At the mention of the word murder, I took the opportunity to bring the conversation round to the young girl. "It's a pity," I said, "that you found no identification on the victim."

"It's as though she fell from the sky," he replied.

"A fallen angel, Inspector?" I asked, a little facetiously.

"Angel? I hardly think so, Mrs. Hudson," he answered in like measure. "In all the years I've been in the business, I've yet to come across an angel, fallen or otherwise. Ah, here we are, the gazebo," he said, pointing to an aging wooden edifice that stood amid a wash of leaves left by its only companion, a giant maple. Beneath the tree stood a constable with horse and cart, alongside a lad about eighteen years of age, at whose feet lay the blanketed body of the victim.

A most somber welcoming committee indeed.

"And how did you get here so quickly, young fellow, m'lad?" asked Thackeray, putting the question to the young man of tousled hair and frightened eyes.

"I ran. Took a short cut, I did. Squire said you wanted to see me and to be right smart about it. So here I am."

"I see. Very commendable on your part, I'm sure," replied the inspector, eyeing the young man up and down. "I only hope that you're as quick and responsive with all your answers."

" 'Ere, what's that supposed to mean? Answers to what?"

Thackeray, ignoring the lad for the moment, turned his attention to me. "Mrs. Hudson, this is Constable McHeath and the lad here, Will Tadlock, groom's helper."

I nodded to the officer and faced the boy. "Tadlock? You're the one who found the body this morning, aren't you?"

The inspector, not the youth, was quick to reply. "Oh, I think he did more than just find her, Mrs. Hudson. It seems our Will was not being all that truthful with us when questioned earlier this morning."

"Told you everything I know, I did!" was young Will's angry and bewildered response.

"Did you! Did you, indeed!" Thackeray snapped back. Then, turning to me, "Perhaps you'll be good enough now, Mrs. Hudson, to tell me of your interest in all this."

I realized it was important that my answer be substantial in nature. He had not granted me permission to view the remains on a whim. I decided it best, if I was to gain his trust and confidence, that I start by invoking the great man's name.

"You've heard of Sherlock Holmes, I take it, Inspector?"

The question took him somewhat aback.

"Holmes? Sherlock Holmes? Yes, of course

I know of him. What officer of the law doesn't? Though I can't say I approve of his methods."

It was now my turn to be taken aback. "Why is that?"

"I don't believe in anyone working outside the law, however honorable their intentions may be. That's why, madam, we have a police force. If everyone was to run about the streets of London, or for that matter, the entire country, trying to solve crimes on their own, we'd be in a fine pickle, wouldn't we? No," he went on, "it's best we leave such things to those who have been trained within the system."

It was hardly the response I would have wished, yet I pressed on. "But, surely," I countered, "you can't dismiss the number of cases he has been responsible for solving?"

"Good heavens, madam! What has Sherlock Holmes have to do with you, at any rate? My question to you—"

"I collaborate with Mr. Holmes," I quietly interjected. My admission, while not totally truthful, could best be described as a lie of elasticity—stretched slightly in my favor.

"You—and Sherlock Holmes!" exclaimed the constable, leaving me to wonder whether his reaction to my announcement was one of awe or disbelief.

His superior, I noted, eyed me rather suspiciously. "Collaborate? Do you, indeed!" said he. "And what would Mr. Holmes and your interest be at Haddley? Surely not the passing of Lady St. Clair—there was no suspicion of foul play in her death. Dr. Morley himself attested to the fact that her ladyship died in her sleep of a heart attack. And," he continued, gazing down upon the blanketed body that lay before him, "the deceased was found but a few short hours ago. Does the great Sherlock Holmes send his operatives on in *advance* of a murder?"

He shook his head in sympathy at what he obviously believed was a poor deluded creature standing before him.

"Inspector Thackeray," I announced, while trying to maintain my composure, "I have reason to believe her ladyship's death was not due to a heart attack. I have reason to believe she was murdered."

"Oh, and why do you believe that, Mrs. Hudson?"

The question was delivered with a wink and a nod toward the constable, who appeared every bit as amused at this ongoing repartee as the inspector. Young Tadlock said nothing throughout the exchange but merely stood there trying to grasp the significance of what he was hearing.

"My reason," I answered, with voice rising in indignation at the cavalier treatment I was receiving, "is . . ."

I stopped.

All I needed now was to tell these two of Violet's out-of-body experience, and I would surely be pronounced mad.

"Mrs. Warner," I announced "has informed me, in no uncertain words, that after entering her ladyship's bedchamber within minutes after, shall we say, her passing, she detected an odor of chloroform within the room."

"I see. Chloroform, you say. Well, we shall certainly make a note of that, never you worry," Thackeray answered, in a patronizing tone. "By the way, Mrs. Hudson," he added, "the other members who were present in the room, they smelled this—this chloroform, did they?"

"Well, no," I sputtered. "At least they said they—"

"I see," he interjected in a condescending tone, "and your Mrs. Warner, that would be the same lady who also saw some sort of mysterious stranger doing her ladyship in, from *outside* the door. Is that right?"

I could do or say nothing but stand there and glower.

"You see, Mrs. Hudson," he continued, in his self-same patronizing manner, "I've done my homework with regard to Mrs. Warner's version of the Saturday night in question."

How smug both he and the constable were. And how I would have liked to have shown my heels to the pair of them. But I was in a man's game and decided to stay the course.

"What does young Tadlock here have to do with your investigation, Inspector? Or is that privileged information?"

"Privileged information? Not at all, madam. At least, not to one who has the good fortune to be a colleague in crime detecting with the renowned Sherlock Holmes. Isn't that right, McHeath?"

"Oh, yes, indeed, sir," replied the subordinate, raising a gloved hand in an effort to conceal the smirk that accompanied the answer.

All right, gentlemen, I thought, play me for the fool, it suits my purposes, not yours.

"As to Tadlock," the inspector began, pausing to take pipe and pouch from pocket, "you may have noticed the private conversation I was engaged in with the squire before taking my leave of that gentleman in escorting you here."

I nodded that I had.

"The gist of the conversation," he informed me, "was that, being unable to sleep last night, the squire rose from his bed and observed the lad crossing the grounds accompanied by a young woman."

He delayed his narrative long enough to tamp tobacco into the bowl and proceeded to light his pipe before continuing.

"They stopped just below that gentleman's window and appeared, from their gestures, to be engaged in some sort of argument."

"Why did the squire not mention this earlier to you?"

"A question I raised myself, madam. His answer being, he had simply forgotten about it when first questioned. It was an incident that lasted but a few moments at best, late at night. It's understandable. I then requested he have the lad meet us here."

"And the squire, he saw nothing else, then?"

"No. By that time, Tadlock and his lady friend had passed from his line of view. As I say, he thought no more about it 'til this morning."

I turned to face the young man. "What do you have to say to all this, Will?"

"It's all a mistake, lady! It weren't the dead girl I were with!"

"Who, then? Speak up!" I urged him. "This is serious business!"

With a deep sigh, he dropped head to chest. "It were Mary."

"Mary?"

"Mary O'Connell," he stated with shoulders that heaved as if a great weight had been lifted from them. "It were she the squire saw me with. Not her," he grimaced, pointing a finger toward the blanketed body.

"Mary O'Connell, was it? Oh, you'll have to do better than that, Sunshine," was the uniformed officer's sardonic reply.

"You've questioned the O'Connell girl, Constable?" asked Thackeray.

"Indeed I have, sir," answered McHeath, withdrawing a pad from the breast pocket of his jacket. "O'Connell, O'Connell," he repeated, while carefully turning over each page. "Ah, here it is. She heard or saw no disturbance of any kind last night," he read, "having gone to bed at quarter past ten. This was confirmed," he added, "by Molly Dwyer, scullery maid. The two share the same sleeping quarters, Inspector," he added, returning the pad to his pocket.

"They're lyin'! The pair of them!" cried the accused.

He took a step back but was checked in retreating any farther by McHeath.

"Why, Will?" I asked. "Why would they lie?"

"I dunno, you ask Mary, Mrs. Hudson. *You* ask her!"

His eyes pleaded with me more eloquently than anything he could have said. The poor wretched creature was caught up in a web not of his own making, of that I was sure.

The senior officer, completely indifferent to the lad's protestations of innocence, requested the constable place the body of the victim on the accompanying wagon before setting off for Twillings where, Tadlock was informed, a formal charge of murder would be brought to bear against him.

"Inspector," I spoke up, "I believe I was granted a request to view the remains."

"Oh, very well, madam," was the reply, accompanied by an exasperated shake of the head. "I wouldn't want your Mr. Holmes to think the Twillings constabulary was not being cooperative in your investigation of a murder. A murder, I might add, that for all intents and purposes, has already been solved!"

I ignored the latter part of his statement and complied with the first.

Easing myself down on one knee, I gently lifted the blanket away from the upper body. What a pretty thing she was. Even in death. And so young, no more than twenty. To have been cut off from life before truly experiencing it was in itself a crime.

The now white alabaster face, framed by the rich chestnut brown of her hair, lay pillowed 'neath the tree on a bed of orange and scarlet.

I offered up a prayer with the thought that if there is an existence of life after death, what better example than the leaves of autumn, now more gloriously alive with a brilliance of color than ever they were in summer's green.

As I gazed deep into that stilled face, a thought that there was something vaguely familiar about this girl kept pushing itself to the forefront of my mind. I quickly brushed the idea aside. Impossible. Certainly there was no one of her age with whom I was acquainted in my small circle of friends. And more's the pity for that, I suppose. Still, like a child tugging at a sleeve for attention, the thought persisted. And then the most extraordinary thing occurred. For one brief instant the word "sailor" flashed through my mind. Sailor? It didn't make sense. I shook my head as if to cast aside these intrusions from what I hoped would be a most clinical and detailed observation.

Like an erupted river of volcanic lava, blood had spewed forth from the back of her head to snake its way through the now matted hair, where it lay in coagulated streams down the side of the face and neck. My curiosity overcame my revulsion when I noticed the pierced left earlobe was devoid of any adornment. I turned her head to one side and, brushing back the hair, discovered an earring in the shape of a half-moon clamped to the right lobe. One earring? If the murder had taken place out here, as the inspector believed, the earring, lost in the ensuing struggle, if I was to follow Thackeray's train of thought, should be no further than my fingertips. My hands moved carefully about, under, and around the fallen leaves. There was, as I had suspected, no sign of its missing companion.

This was not a local girl. Nor a gypsy, as had been the colonel's hypothesis. Not from what I could see of her clothes from beneath the half-opened coat. Inexpensive, mind you, but fashionable. A Londoner? Oh, if only I had more time. But a series of coughs coupled with intermittent clearings of the throat by the good inspector was an indication to me of his impatience. I gently turned the open portion of the blanket back over the body and took note on rising that from the heel of each shoe lay a line of indentation extending across the soft wet ground to the edge of the path. Had not Thackeray noticed the obvious? If so, he gave no indication to me.

I concluded the inspector was not about to concern himself with anything that might alter his already preconceived theory. Tadlock plus girl, plus argument, equaled murder. All ship-shape in Bristol fashion. As for myself, I could not believe it was all that simple an equation. This blinders-on attitude taken by an inspector, late of the London police, led me to speculate as to whether his move from city to shire was entirely of his own choosing.

"If you are quite finished . . ." spoke the inspector in a bored monotone.

I nodded politely.

He turned to McHeath. "You may now place the body on the wagon, Constable. You, there, Tadlock, give the officer a hand." Then turning to me, "The path will lead you back, Mrs. Hudson. Unless, of course, you want me—"

"Thank you, no, Inspector," I replied. "I shall find my way with no trouble. Thank you again, for indulging an old woman's request."

"Before taking your leave, Mrs. Hudson, one question, please. I'd be interested to know what, in your professional opinion, are your findings regarding the body of the deceased?"

The question was asked with an all too obvious emphasis on the word "professional."

Two could play that tune. "I found she had been murdered," I replied, facetiously.

The poor man looked quite askance, no doubt wondering if it was he who was now being played for the fool.

"The question remains, Inspector," I added, "murdered by whom?"

"By Will Tadlock!" he snapped. "What you don't seem to understand, madam, is that this is not some sort of game I'm playing here!"

"My dear Inspector," said I, feeling not in the least intimidated by his sudden outburst, "life itself is a game. Why should it not be so in death?"

Bushy eyebrows knitted together as his two beady eyes burned into mine for what seemed the longest time. I received a curt, "Good day to you, madam," followed by a perfunctory tip of the bowler as he turned with a purposeful stride toward the cart. With the constable now at the reins and Will sitting dejectedly in back, the inspector clambered aboard. As they set off on their journey to Twillings, the young lad cried out to me in a pleading tone, "Help me, Mrs. Hudson. You believe me, I know you do!"

Help him? I only wished that I could. "I'll try, Will Tadlock. I'll try," I called back with a smile that belied my doubts.

As they disappeared into the distance I made one last desperate search for the missing earring by carefully examining the ground on which the body had lain. Unfortunately, I found nothing. With a sigh, I raised myself up and, noting that the once gentle smattering of rain was now developing into a full-blown storm, I quickly placed my shawl over my head and made a quick retreat back to Haddley.

NINE

A Private Conversation

"THEY'VE LEFT THEN, have they, Hogarth?" I asked, on seeing the old gentleman closing the door of the music room behind him.

"Not more than five minutes ago, Mrs. Hudson."

"Mrs. Warner, as well?"

He nodded that she had, adding, "She asked me to tell you she would see you at dinner, if not before."

I rested a forefinger at the base of my chin and stared at the floor, a habit I'm told I have when puzzled or deep in thought.

"Forgive me, Hogarth," I said, returning my attention to the old gentleman, "but I'm somewhat surprised to see you did not accompany the family and staff to the funeral service."

"I thought it best, madam, that someone remain at Haddley during the absence of the family." He paused, wondering no doubt whether I was entitled to any further explanation before remarking, "I shall, in any event, visit the gravesite to privately pay my respects at a more convenient time."

I was relieved that he had expanded upon his statement for I believed it showed he was not adverse to being more open with me than he or his position would normally allow. A good sign. I needed his confidence.

I settled myself down on a richly upholstered and extremely comfortable redleather chesterfield. Patting the seat of the cushion next to me, I asked, "Would I be breaking any rule of social decorum if I requested you sit with me, so that we might have ourselves a little chat?" The old gentleman appeared quite taken aback by my request. After a moment or two of flustered hesitation, he at last eased himself down beside me.

"So you've elected to stay behind, have you—like a captain who refuses to leave his ship," was my lighthearted opening.

"Madam speaks in the jargon of one who is acquainted with the sea," was the stiff and formal reply.

I answered that both my husband and my father had spent the better part of their lives before the mast, adding that my father and his ship were lost in a storm during a run from the Dutch East Indies to London.

The aged face softened in sympathy on hearing the tale. "I'm sorry to hear that, Mrs. Hudson. What line did he sail with?"

That he would ask what line revealed a knowledge of maritime shipping that surprised me.

"Blackwell," I answered.

The old head nodded knowingly. "Blackwell," he mused. "Yes, a good company. I myself crewed on the *Thomas B. Henly*, a windjammer of the Blackwell line—to the West Indies and back. Our cargo being, as I recall, rum and sugar cane."

He had taken me completely by surprise. Who would have guessed this kindly, frail old man seated next to me at one time climbed rigging, unfurled canvas, and felt ocean spray? How quick we are to compartmentalize people into our own preconceived notion of what they are, have been, or should be.

"And yet," I answered, "here you are at Haddley."

Adjusting himself into a more comfortable position, he answered with a wry smile, "Before you go taking me for an old salt, Mrs. Hudson, I must confess it was my one and only excursion with life on the open sea. My father, you see," he continued in a more relaxed vein, "served all his life at Haddley, as did his father before him. But with the exuberance of youth, I decided if I was to serve, it would be at sea. A far more glamorous and adventurous life it seemed, than padding about carpeted floors."

I nodded knowingly, said nothing, and let him continue.

"But I'm afraid," he went on, "I learned all too soon a sailor's life was not for me. Sick, madam. Sick, the entire voyage. I vowed if ever again I saw England, never more would I stray from the hallowed halls of Haddley."

I gently patted the white-gloved hand. "Still, all in all . . ." I said, my voice trailing off.

"Yes, still, all in all," was the quiet response, "I would not have missed it for the world."

"It would seem," I smiled, "we share a common link with the sea, you and I."

He turned to me and for the first time, I thought, saw not merely a visitor to Haddley before him but the face of a friend. At that moment I believed a bond was established between us. I thought it now time to take a more direct approach. "Hogarth," I asked, "would I be amiss in thinking you did not attend her ladyship's funeral due to some, shall we say, private dislike of the family?"

I received a raised eyebrow, a smile, and a noncommittal reply. "There's more to you than meets the eye, Mrs. Hudson."

I returned the smile.

Slowly, the sparse body eased itself back against leather while thoughtful eyes stared deep into time and space before I was, at last, rewarded with an answer.

"Oh, I don't dislike the lads, that is to say, Sir Charles and the squire. Good heavens, I remember when they were born! Those were indeed happy times," he added, more, I think, to himself than to me.

"And these gentlemen—now?"

"From my own personal standpoint, I would say 'disappointed' would be the appropriate word."

"Disappointed? In what way?"

"The drinking with the one and the gambling with the other," he quietly replied, while methodically brushing away imaginary flecks of lint from his lapel. A gesture, I thought, he hoped would imply a certain casualness on his part in attempting to cover his embarrassment in relating a failure of character on the part of his employers.

"Both gentlemen," I remarked, to let him know I was not altogether uninformed with respect to the St. Clairs, "spend a great deal of their time in London, I believe."

"Yes, quite true. In fact, their unexpected arrival from London last week had the staff in quite a dither."

Ah, I thought, here was something on which to hang my hat. As I recall, a maxim of Mr. Holmes had been that any deviation from a normal pattern, as would be the case in unannounced arrivals, while not in itself suspect, should at least warrant a full inspection. I felt it was now time to jot down a timetable of sorts with regard to all parties concerned.

"Hogarth," I asked, "could I possibly trouble you for a sheet of paper and a pencil?"

"Certainly, Mrs. Hudson, no trouble at all," he replied, rising up and making his way over to a small desk.

"Thank you, Hogarth," I said as he handed me a writing tablet and pencil on his return.

As he resumed his place beside me I jotted down the line—"Lady St. Clair: Death occurred Saturday night." After reading back aloud I noted that the old gentleman was eyeing me with some trepidation.

"Yes, Hogarth?" I asked as his gloved hand tugged nervously at his collar.

"These—notes of yours, Mrs. Hudson," he asked, eyeing the paper, "for what purpose are they intended?"

It is quite true I hadn't been all that open with him, and it was quite right that he should question me with respect to my intentions.

"Mrs. Warner and I," I informed him, "are conducting our own investigation into the tragic events of these last few days. You, Hogarth, could be most helpful to the both of us. Of course," I added, to establish a credibility of purpose, "any information we are fortunate to discover will naturally be made known to the police." I held my breath and awaited his reply.

"I shall, of course, be glad to assist you in any way I can. If only in respect to the memory of both Lord and Lady St. Clair," he assured me.

I heaved a sigh of relief.

"Now then," I began, "you say the baronet and the squire arrived back at the estate unexpectedly. Is that right?"

"And Lady Margaret, as well."

I'm afraid I appeared a trifle perplexed. "The three journeyed to London, then?"

"No, madam," the old butler replied, with a sympathetic smile. "Let me explain. Lady Margaret, Sir Charles, and Squire left Haddley a week ago Monday. Both gentlemen to London on business, Lady Margaret to Devon to visit her mother. Do you follow me?"

"Yes, yes," I answered, putting pencil to paper with respect to the facts as they unfolded. "Go on."

"On Friday morning last, this being no more than five days after his departure, and three days earlier than he had been expected, I was startled to learn from Cook that the squire had returned and requested breakfast be brought to his room."

"Then he must have arrived late Thursday night or early Friday morning," I replied, thoughtfully tapping pencil to chin.

"It would appear so. Although neither the staff nor I had seen him enter. Then that same Friday, Sir Charles returned as I was about to retire for the night. I expressed my surprise and informed him his brother had also returned unexpectedly."

"What did he say to that?"

"He appeared genuinely surprised."

"And Lady Margaret, what time . . . ?"

"Saturday morning. Shortly before noon."

"And no explanation was given by either one for this sudden return to the roost?"

"To me? Good heavens, no, madam! Nor would it be in my place to ask."

"I see. Yes, of course. As for Colonel Wyndgate," I asked, while endeavoring to write smaller and smaller as space gave way to copy, "he remained here, did he?"

"The colonel? Oh, yes. Never strays too far from Haddley, does our colonel." Then, as an afterthought, he added, "It must be a lonely life for the old soldier."

"But a comfortable one," I remarked, somewhat sarcastically on glancing enviously about at the opulent ambience of our surroundings. "And when did the good doctor make his appearance on the scene?" I asked, returning my thoughts back to the business at hand.

"On Saturday evening, a little after eight o'clock, as I recall. It being either the baronet or the squire who sent for him."

"Why was that?"

"From what I was given to understand, Lady St. Clair had been complaining of dizzy spells. Dr. Morley had her put to bed. Sir Charles requested he stay on a few more days to keep an eye on her. 'Pon my word," he exclaimed as I returned to my writing, "do you know, I've never before spoken so openly to anyone with regard to the family? That is to say, not since Mrs. Hogarth passed away. She was, you know, housekeeper here at Haddley."

I replied I hadn't known and expressed my regrets on her passing.

"Thank you, Mrs. Hudson, but that was a long time ago. His lordship was alive then, and what a fine old gentleman he was, too. I don't mind telling you," he continued, with no little pride, "it was he who paid for all the hospital expenses during Mrs. Hogarth's illness—yes, and the funeral, as well. And many's the time I'd see Lady St. Clair, herself, sitting quietly by my missus's bedside, comforting her during those final days," he added with a sigh in remembrance of it all.

I'm afraid I intruded upon his reverie by bringing him up to the present, in asking, "You were with Mrs. Warner in the bedroom on the night of her ladyship's death, weren't you, Hogarth?"

"What? Oh, yes." There was a slight pause before he quietly uttered the word, "Odd."

I seized on the word. "Odd? In what way, odd?"

"It's hard to explain, madam. But I sensed something was not quite right. But then, perhaps I'm making more of this than I ought."

"Not necessarily," I replied. "You know, of course, Mrs. Warner also believes as you do."

I left it at that without going into Vi's astral excursions.

"Oh, yes," he answered, raising a gloved hand in a polite attempt to cover a smile. "She was, as I recall, quite vocal in her belief that some sort of mysterious intruder had invaded her ladyship's bedroom and done her in." Then in a more serious vein, "But I should tell you that Mrs. Warner, for whom I have the greatest respect, mind you, is quite mistaken. There was no other person in the room—other than we two and the poor dead woman, herself."

"Someone could have been hiding . . ."

"No," he stated quite firmly. "The St. Clairs, Dr. Morley, and Colonel Wyndgate entered the room almost immediately after our arrival. There was no else present. I'm sorry, Mrs. Hudson."

Even with his statement that he had seen no one, it did not alter my belief in Vi one whit. I'm a stubborn old goat, and I was now more determined than ever to prove her right. Still, I was left in a confused state of mind.

Hogarth noted my frustration. "Ah, madam, these are terrible days indeed, for all of us," he sighed, brushing a finger under the lashes of a rheumy eye. "And now we have a poor girl murdered on the very grounds of the estate, itself. I'm only thankful his lordship is not alive to see all this."

"Things will right themselves in the end," I assured him, although at that particular moment I could have used some reassurance myself.

As I did not wish to prolong his depression, I thought it as good a time as any to ask if he would indulge me in a request.

"Yes, of course, Mrs. Hudson," he answered. "What is it you wish?"

Before directly responding, I recounted to him the events that had taken place the night before when I'd been awakened by cries, groans, and argumentative voices. And, being in a state of drowsiness, due to the lateness of the hour, it was not all that clear to me where the sounds had emanated from. "Although," I added, "I am of the opinion it would be the room directly above Mrs. Warner's."

"The top floor?"

"Yes. That puzzles you?"

"It's just that the rooms on that level have not been used as living quarters for well over a century and a half, I should say."

"They remain empty?"

"For the most part. Although a number of them are used as storage areas, I believe. But it's been a good number of years since I was up there." Then with a self-disparaging smile, he added, "It's enough for these old legs of mine to climb the great staircase. In any event, what you heard was probably no more than the creaks and groans associated with any old structure, be it house or human." He chuckled.

"Perhaps." I smiled. "Still, if I'm right, there could be something up there that would shed some light on the mystery of who the dead girl was and why she was murdered."

"I don't understand," he replied, looking a trifle perplexed. "She died outside—not within the manor."

"Did she? Did she, indeed, Hogarth? I wonder."

"I'm afraid all this is too much for me to grasp," he stated with a sigh and a weary shake of that aged head. "But, about this favor you mentioned, what exactly—?"

"I should like to do a little investigating up there," I informed him. "And I'll need the keys to those rooms."

"I really shouldn't, you know," he replied, wagging a finger at me as would a teacher to a naughty child. "But how could an old sea dog like me refuse the daughter of a former ship's captain?" The question was asked rhetorically and, I might add, with a touch of whimsy. "Although what you hope to find up there," he added, "I don't know."

"Nor I. In any event, it's a beginning."

"I keep the keys in a special place. For security reasons—the household staff, you understand, I'm sure," he whispered. Though why he whispered, I had no idea, for as far as

I knew, we were the only living souls in the house. But such was his sense of responsibility, I assumed he felt a hushed and confidential manner was appropriate to the occasion. "Although," he continued, "I see no reason to keep the secret from you. They're in the kitchen, actually, atop the—the kitchen!" he gasped. "Bless my soul, Mrs. Hudson—do forgive me!"

"Why, whatever for?"

"Why, dear lady, you've not eaten all day, have you?"

"Just a bun with tea this morning," I answered meekly.

"Yes, yes, well, that will never do. Come along."

I stood up and discreetly offered my arm in assisting him to a standing position.

"But not a word to Cook when she returns, mind you," he said, closing the door to the study behind us. "Why, even Lady Margaret herself would think twice before invading the sacrosanct kingdom of Cook's kitchen."

"Then Cook must be quite formidable, indeed!" I laughed.

"As you might express it, Mrs. Hudson, the kitchen is her ship and she, the captain. But," he added, with a wink, "I don't think she'll miss a bit of roast beef and a slice of pie."

"Speaking of Lady Margaret, as we were, and the baronet too, for that matter, are there no children by their marriage?" I asked, as we proceeded along a carpetless and dimly lit hallway that I presumed was used primarily by the servants.

It was a question I should have thought to ask Vi, but nevertheless, I now had a deeper well of information at my elbow on which to draw.

"Yes, one son," he answered. "And a fine lad he is too. At Cambridge now. Last year for him, I believe."

"And the squire—he never married?"

"Oh, yes. An elopement, actually. Bit of a scandal there, as I recall."

I started to speak but a gloved hand was raised in admonition.

"Don't ask the whys or wherefores of it, Mrs. Hudson. No one, at least, we, the servants, ever did know the reason behind it all." The gloved hand came down. "That's not to say," he continued, "that gossip did not run rampant among the staff."

"I can well imagine."

Still, I was skeptical of his being as unaware of the events as he would have me believe, and I refused to let it end there. "But surely Hogarth," I asked in gentle persistence, "in your capacity as a valued and trusted servant, you would be more knowledgeable with respect to, as you put it, the whys and wherefores, than other members of the household staff, would you not?"

His reply was not immediately forthcoming, and I could see, while being flattered by my acknowledging his status, he felt ill at ease in being asked to dredge up a private incident from the family's past.

"I will say this," he replied thoughtfully, "there was some mention of his wife being given a certain amount of money with the proviso she book passage to either Australia or Canada."

"But why?"

"She was not of the same social standing. A working girl, she was, from the village."

"Whose idea was this, then?"

"For her to leave? Lady St. Clair's. She was quite adamant about it, as I recall. Although, you must understand," he added hastily, in defense of his late employer, "it was not done out of malice on her ladyship's part. It's just that the aristocracy live within a different social structure than we. You understand."

I nodded all too knowingly as I continued my questioning. "And the squire—he agreed to all this?"

"He was given a choice. To remain at Haddley or to make a new life for his wife and himself overseas. For the squire, the choice was obvious. He chose to remain here."

"Were there any children by this union?"

"One child. A girl. It was understood she would remain here, to be brought up at Haddley. But it was a bargain not kept by the mother."

"How long ago was all this, then?"

He pondered the question for a moment or two. "I should say," he answered at last, "no more than twenty years, at best."

"And the squire's wife and the daughter have never been seen since?"

"Never. Although at one time letters would

arrive postmarked Canada." A pause. "Or was it Australia? In any event," he continued, "Mrs. Hogarth and I assumed they were from the squire's wife."

Then, in the realization as to the wealth of information he had just imparted, unwittingly or otherwise, the venerable old gentleman implored me, in no uncertain terms, to keep what I had heard in the strictest confidence. When I responded by giving him my utmost assurance that I would, a quiet and profound sense of relief swept over him.

We continued our walk in silence until I was asked by Hogarth if the information I was now privy to would in any way be beneficial to my investigation.

"At this point," I replied, sighing a weary sigh, "everything is food for thought."

"Ah, speaking of food, Mrs. Hudson," announced my newfound confidant as we approached a door at the end of the hall, "the kitchen awaits."

All thoughts of further questions faded away as visions of roast beef danced in my head.

TEN

The Room Upstairs

❧WITH KEY IN one hand, candle in the other, a handbag hanging from my wrist, and a feeling of trepidation within, I cautiously made my way down a seemingly never-ending hallway bathed in blackness and foreboding.

Remembering Hogarth had mentioned it had been over a century and a half since the upstairs area of the great house had been occupied, I felt I had entered a time tunnel where, at any moment, a door would suddenly be flung open by a vaporous apparition from the seventeenth century demanding an explanation as to my unwarranted presence.

As it was, I took small comfort in the realization that my shadow, distorted in size and form by the flickering flame, was my only companion. How I wished, within my heart of hearts, that Vi was at my side.

If the voices that awakened me had indeed come from the room above Violet's, the door before which I now stood should by all accounts be the one I sought. I pressed my ear against it and listened—why, I really don't know. I suppose it was a natural reaction, for I found it hard to believe anyone would still be in there.

"Please, Lord," I said, offering up a silent prayer, "if there is, let them be alive." My constitution being such, I could only endure the viewing of one corpse per day.

In went the key.

I turned the handle and was surprised to find how effortlessly it swung open on its hinges. No creaking door here—a silent tribute to the quality of craftsmanship from an earlier age.

I stood timidly at the threshold with door ajar.

As daylight slowly absorbed itself into evening, the fading light tried with partial success to penetrate a multipaned, grime-laden window, located at the far end of the room. The limited light it afforded, coupled with that of the candle, was enough for me to see a room stacked high with great wooden crates and boxes of various shapes and sizes. Objets d'art and numerous gilt-framed paintings lay abandoned on sheet-covered sofas, divans, chesterfields, and chairs. A grayish nightmare of a room, blanketed in dust from decades past.

Good Lord! I thought, gazing at the artifacts before me, this place is a miniature museum. Great treasures such as these should be properly displayed. To be left to a viewing public consisting of rats, mice, and spiders is intolerable!

Now, more annoyed than frightened, I wondered whether it was worth my while to enter, when, by happenstance, I glanced downward and was startled to see on the dust-laden floor the unmistakable sign of footprints, clearly enough defined for me to distinguish the prints were made by shoes belonging to both sexes.

In I went, following the trail as easily as would a hunter tracking a jackrabbit over freshly powdered snow. I continued around a maze of boxes and cartons until the telltale path ended behind a large wooden crate that served as a walled partition for the iron cot behind it. It would have been obvious, even to Thackeray, that the last person to lay a head upon that cot with its rumpled sheets and crumpled pillow had resided in this century, not the last.

There was now no doubt in my mind this was the room the voices had emanated from the night before. A hairpin caught my eye as it lay half-hidden 'neath the pillow. A bottle of wine, three quarters of it consumed, stood upon a small table placed beside the cot. A glass that had fallen on its side lay gazing down at its shattered companion on the floor below.

On examining the window I saw that a small area of grime had been rubbed away from the corner of the pane, allowing a partial view of the grounds below. As I stood there, a small gray mouse, completely indifferent to

my presence, paused long enough at my feet
to nibble away at a crumb before scurrying off
into the shadows. Picking up the remainder of
his meal, I saw it to be pastry crumb, stale, of
course, but not by a hundred and fifty years.

So, here our mysterious occupant had
stayed, slept, and ate with nothing to indicate
that she, for it could have been no other than
the poor dead girl herself, had been an un-
willing guest. Certainly, if she had wanted to
scream out against a prolonged and forced
captivity, her cries would have been heard.
Then why had she remained here? And for
how long? More than twenty-four hours, of
that I was sure by the remainder of a meal and
the brown-skinned apple cores that lay strewn
over a small table set to the side of the bed.
But why was she hidden away in an unused
room? And by whose request? I was only now
realizing that criminal investigations could be
quite a frustrating occupation.

I placed the candle on the table, and, getting
down on both knees, ran a hand blindly across
the floor under the cot, in the hope my fingers
would feel out what my eyes could not see. If
I could but find the mate to the earring worn
by that poor unfortunate creature, it would be
proof, admissable in any court of law, as op-
posed to merely my own supposition, that the
murdered victim had been residing at the estate before her untimely death. Alas, there was
no such earring to be found.

However, my hand did engage upon a object of a much larger dimension. Withdrawing
it, I saw I had retrieved a marble statuette of

a cherub no more than eighteen inches in height. Placing it carefully on the table, I rested myself on the cot and moved the candle closer to my find. And there I sat, spellbound by the outward beauty of an innocent babe bathed in the soft glow of candlelight, its eyes gazing heavenward, with little arms outstretched in joy and adoration, as if welcoming the Creator Himself into its presence. As I moved the base slowly around, the better to admire this exquisite example of what I believed to be fifteenth-century sculpture, I was dismayed to discover an imperfection on the side of the head and extending down the back of the body. It piqued my interest to the extent that I moved the candle closer for a more detailed inspection. It appeared as if the little angel had suffered a mortal blow to the head and the dark reddish-brown stain marring its perfection was blood that had flowed from the wound.

Looking back, I suppose it was my analogy of blood to stain that brought me back to reality. However gifted that artisan of centuries past, not even Michelangelo could have created life inside that marbled body. Oh, it was blood, to be sure. Closer inspection told me that much. But not from the cherub.

The closer inspection I allude to relates to my use of Mr. Holmes's magnifying glass. Or, at least, one in a series of such glasses that gentleman had acquired over the years. Should Mr. H ever read the lines I now set down, he can rest assured the said item has long since been returned to his small chest of drawers atop the walnut cabinet by the window. The only explanation I can offer for the taking of it is that since I would be representing him, as it were, at Haddley, I felt the item in question, with which he has long been associated, offered me a certain sense of professionalism. A fortuitous piece of happenstance, in any event, for on removing it from my hand bag, I found its magnification enabled a pair of tired eyes to distinguish the presence of fine strands of hair embedded within the stain on the statue.

Carefully picking up the marbled babe and cradling it in my arms, as would a mother with child, I made my way from the scene of the murder, mentally congratulating myself on having found the blunt instrument, attributable to the death of the young woman whose remains I had viewed only that morning.

After dinner, Vi and I, passing on a dessert of iced sherbet, discreetly withdrew from the table and took ourselves into the study.

"That were about as merry a meal as the Last Supper, that were!" spoke my companion, shifting her weight in the chair opposite me. "Got so, I'd 'ave even welcomed a word or two from the old colonel. Great twit though he is."

"I suppose," I answered, "the lack of conversation was understandable. It hasn't been the most pleasant of days for any of us."

"Aye, especially for them—if they've got any conscience at all. Should have seen Lady Margaret at the service, Em. Sobbin' away, she was, and dabbin' her eyes like she were that heartbroken. Why, you'd 'ave thought she were attendin' the funeral of Father Christmas! Aye, and I'll tell you summat else," she added, wagging a finger in my direction. "It wouldn't surprise me none if it were Lady High-and-Mighty herself that done me mistress in."

"It's easy enough," I countered, "to point suspicion at someone you've little regard for, but that does not necessarily mean Lady Margaret is guilty of anything, save for a most disagreeable manner."

"Right enough, I suppose," she answered with a sigh. "But, 'ere," she said, fixing her attention on me, "what's your opinion as to all these goin's on, eh?"

"None," I confessed. "Other than, in a matter of two days we have been confronted with not one but two murders which, for all we know, may or may not be related."

"I see," she answered with yet another sigh. "Then we're no better off than we were before—right?"

"I wouldn't go so far as to say that," I replied. "I believe my findings this afternoon have helped me in establishing a foundation of evidence from which we can now build."

"*Your* findings! This afternoon? What's this all about, eh? Thought you stayed behind so's to have yourself a little nap, I did."

I apologized for not informing her earlier of my activities, but as I pointed out, this was my first real opportunity since her return from the funeral to actually sit down and discuss the events of the day as they had unfolded.

I related in detail my examination of the murdered girl's body, Will Tadlock's subsequent arrest, the hidden room where the victim had stayed, and my finding the blood-stained cherub, which I would later produce for her from its hiding place beneath the folded clothes in the bottom drawer of her dresser.

She listened with open-mouthed astonishment without so much as one word of interruption until the tale was told, before remarking, "You *have* been busy—I'll say that much! Why, Mr. Holmes would be ever so proud of you, he would."

While flattered, any response I might have made, humble or otherwise, was left unspoken by her continuance.

"And poor Will, arrested for murder!" she exclaimed. "Why, he'd no more hurt a fly than you or I. And fancy him and Mary. Meetin' on the sly, you say?"

"If you can believe the young man, they did. Did the girl ever mention to you she was seeing him?"

"No. Nary a word. But it's not like Will to lie. Not that he's all that honest, mind you. It's just he's not all that clever, if you get my drift."

"Yet Mary says she never saw him last night."

"Well, don't look at me," she replied in exasperation. "I don't know what to make of it all."

"Nor I," I answered. "Which is why I took the opportunity earlier of asking Hogarth to have the girl join us after we had finished our meal." With the old butler having mentioned that the family, along with the colonel and the doctor, always made a habit of retiring to the music room after dining, I thought the safest place to set up a meeting with Mary would be here in the study.

"Seems like you and Hogarth hit it off right proper, from what you've been telling me. Bit old for you though, ain't he, luv?"

"Oh, Vi, really!" Anything further I could have added was interrupted by a tap at the door.

"The O'Connell girl!" I whispered excitedly. "I think it would best suit our purpose if we pretend to know more than we do, when questioning her."

"Pretend to know—?"

"Shhh! Just go along with me."

A comely girl, no more than twenty, if that, dressed in the obligatory black dress and white apron with lace cap perched atop an up-swept hairdo, timidly entered the room with a knowing smile to Vi and a questioning look toward me.

"Mrs. Hudson, is it? I was told it was me you'd be wantin' to see."

"Yes, Mary," I answered warmly. "Mrs. Warner and I would like to have a little chat, if we may, with you." I gestured, with a wave of my hand, to the chair on my left. "Please, sit down."

She hesitated, looking to Vi for guidance as to whether it would be within keeping of her situation.

"Sit down, Mary, that's a good girl," announced my old friend with a friendly smile. "Don't wait for an opportunity to take the weight off your feet, I always say."

No sooner had she complied with my request than she began fidgeting in her chair as would a student brought before the headmaster. As we were now at eye level, I was taken aback to see a certain resemblance between her and the murdered girl.

Dear Lord, I thought, as memories of my late husband being haunted by the faces of his dead shipmates flashed through my mind, am I now to be subjected to seeing that poor dead girl in the face of every young woman?

"Would there be anything wrong, Mrs. Hudson?"

"What?"

Lost deep in thought, I hadn't realized my staring, though innocent as it was of any rudeness on my part, was causing her undue embarrassment.

"No, no. Nothing," I smiled. "But tell me," I asked, "where is it you call home?"

An innocuous question at best, but put forward in the hope of establishing a repartee of sorts before easing the conversation into a more serious vein.

"Home? County Clare, Mrs. Hudson."

"County Clare," I repeated. "Even the name has a lilt to it. It must be very lovely there."

"Lovely, is it? That's somethin' I'd not be knowin' about."

"Oh." I didn't know quite what else to say.

"A body doesn't get much of a chance to be

admirin' the scenery when you're the eldest of
eight, missus. Worked hard all me life, I have.
What with me father havin' died and me
mother, darlin' woman that she is, though
never knowin' a day without somethin' ailin'
her, I was left to look after the lot of 'em!
Cookin', washin', scrubbin', with never a day
to meself. Look," she exclaimed, extending
both arms out before us, "nineteen, I am, with
the hands of an old woman! Oh," she stammered, with cheeks of blushed red, "bless me,
madam, I didn't mean . . ."

A smile from the two elderly ladies.

" 'Ere, now, never you mind, Mary," responded my companion with a chuckle. "Em
and I are under no illusions we'll ever be
called upon to be queen of the May at this
stage of our lives."

"And so you came to England to seek your
fortune," said I, still smiling over Vi's last remark.

"It's not for the likes of me to be thinkin' of
fortunes, Mrs. Hudson. An honest day's wage
for an honest day's work is all I can ask or
hope for."

"And Haddley Hall—you like it well
enough here, do you?"

"Well enough."

She left me an opening, and I sailed right in.
"And Will Tadlock, you like him well enough,
too?"

The mouth dropped open as the eyes wid-
ened in confusion and surprise. She shifted
uncomfortably in her chair, turning first to Violet and then to me. "Will Tadlock? I'd not be

knowin' what you mean, Mrs. Hudson, and that's the truth of it."

"Oh, come now, Mary, you and Will—it's common knowledge." I flashed a glance toward Violet. "Isn't that right, Mrs. Warner?"

"Aye, right enough," she replied, stepping in to give credence to the lie. "It weren't no secret to me. Nor others I could mention."

"Others, you say!" she exclaimed, gripping both arms of the chair with fingers digging deep into fabric. "B-but Lady Margaret," she stammered, "she'd not be knowin', would she?"

"No," said I, "she, at least, knows nothing." Which, in all probability, was true in any case.

Her body, that only moments before she held as rigid as any yeoman of the guard, suddenly collapsed like a rag doll with an overwhelming sense of relief.

"Praise be for that!" she exclaimed.

My companion and I exchanged curious glances.

"Why this concern of yours regarding Lady Margaret?" I asked.

There was no response.

We sat in silence until quite unexpectedly the young woman arose to her feet. "If that's all you'll be wantin', Mrs. Hudson, Mrs. Warner, I'd best be gettin' back to me duties."

I found myself momentarily stunned by her unexpected curtailment of the conversation. But before letting her sail out the room, I waded in with the hope of disarming her defenses.

"I don't think you realize the severity of the

situation," I began, as she turned from me to the door. "Squire St. Clair has told Inspector Thackeray of seeing Will and a young woman on the grounds of the estate last night. Will says it was you. The inspector, thanks to your testimony of being asleep at the time in question, has disregarded his story. It is his belief that Will Tadlock was in the company of the girl who was murdered. I'm sorry, Mary, but I think you should know your young man was arrested earlier this morning on suspicion of murder. And, I'm afraid, the lad is at this very moment residing in a cell at Twillings."

With a face now as white as the apron she wore, she staggered back a few steps, clutching a hand to her mouth as if to stifle a scream, while her body swayed dizzily from side to side. I feared she was about to faint.

"Quick, Vi, catch her!" I cried.

Before either of us had a chance to move, she fell back into the chair, her body heaving in uncontrollable grief.

"Will, arrested for murder! But, he's innocent, he is, Mrs. Hudson. I swear by all the blessed saints in heaven!" she cried, tears welling up within those blue Irish eyes.

"Then it *was* you he was with last night," I stated.

She confirmed as much in between heart-wrenching sobs.

"There, there, Mary," said I, leaning over with a gentle pat to her hand, "there's no need for you to be upsetting yourself."

I gave her a moment or two to collect herself before asking if she felt up to helping me reconstruct the events of the previous night.

She withdrew a small linen handkerchief from under her sleeve, blew her nose, and did her best to summon up a smile.

"You left your room last night, walking from the manor to Will's quarters above the stable. Would that be right?"

I received a nod of affirmation.

"At about what time?"

" 'Bout eleven, I suppose. But I didn't stay long."

" 'Til when, then?"

"It'd be no more than a little after twelve."

"You came back alone?"

"Alone? No. Will walked me back. He didn't as a rule, but last night, we had, well, a bit of a lover's spat, you might say. He followed me back trying to soothe things over with those honey words of his."

"But, in fact," I pressed her, "you continued your spat right up to the door, didn't you?"

"I'm afraid we did, at that."

"Confirming," I said, exchanging a triumphant smile with Violet, "Will's story and the events as the squire saw it!"

"But Mary," questioned Vi, "why did you lie about it, luv?"

"Because of Lady Margaret," she began, dabbing those now red-rimmed eyes with the corner of her apron. "She had a rule, you see. There'd be no . . . no"—she paused—"fraternization?" she asked.

"Fraternization, yes."

"Fraternization between the help—men and women, if you know what I mean. One of the

first things I was told when I started here, she
wanted no funny business goin' on at Haddley
with the servants and all. If her ladyship ever
found out 'bout Will and me, I'd be out within
the hour, bag and baggage. And that's the
truth of it."

"But would that have been so terrible?" I
asked.

"Terrible, she says!" Her eyes flashed wide
in disbelief that I would have thought to even
ask such a question. "And me with seven
brothers and sisters and a dyin' mother to look
after! It's what little money I can send home
from me wages what's keepin' 'em alive!"

"Oh, we are sorry," announced my companion. "Well, I mean, we didn't know, did we?"

"Then that's why," I said, stepping in, "the
other girl. Molly—?"

"Molly Dwyer."

"Yes, Molly Dwyer. That's why you had her
go along with you on your story to the constable. You were afraid of losing your position."

"And Molly," questioned Mary, "she'll not
be gettin' into any trouble, will she?"

I answered that as I intended to pay the
good inspector a call on the morrow, I'd do
what I could in putting things right. And now
that the truth of her and Will's liaison could
be substantiated, I assured her the police
would have no alternative but to release him.

At that, Vi and I were subjected to an outburst of gratitude from a deliriously happy
young colleen who, before taking her leave,
turned to us in a hopeful yet hesitant manner.

"Lady Margaret," she stammered, "she doesn't—that is—she wouldn't have to—"

"Oh, never you mind about her," Violet reassured her. "She'll hear nowt from us."

Before closing the door behind her, two elderly ladies were rewarded with a smile as wide as the Irish Sea.

ELEVEN

Mrs. Warner Comes A-Calling

‸MY COMPANION, SLIPPING into her nightgown, whilst absent-mindedly humming a merry little melody to herself, seemed in the highest of spirits as she made ready for bed.

"I don't mind tellin' you, Em, it's that pleased I am," said she, fluffing out the pillows with a few well-placed thumps.

"Pleased?"

"Aye. What with our solvin' of the murder, and all."

I've always tried to expect the unexpected from my old friend, but this time she caught me completely off-guard. "Solving the . . .? My dear, Mrs. Warner, we've solved no murder."

"Well, we know now it weren't Will Tadlock, right?"

"Violet, Violet, Violet," I repeated, in exasperation. "I believe the object of the investigation is to find out who did it—not who didn't."

"Ah, well, that's you, isn't it? Always seein' the bottle as bein' half-empty."

I smiled. She was right, of course, at least to the extent we had made progress. I sat down on the corner of the bed and silently watched as she puttered about her dresser, humming contentedly to herself.

"What's that?" I asked.

"What's what?"

"That tune you're humming. It sounds familiar."

"Don't see how it could be," she answered. "It's just summat I heard Sir Charles plunkin' away at on the piano once or twice. And you know me, Em, always did have an ear for music."

"And yet, I know that tune," I said, becoming quite frustrated at this lapse of memory on my part. "Could it be something from Gilbert and Sullivan?"

"Gilbert and Sullivan? Not ruddy likely. I'd of known it if it was, what with me musical background, and all. Took piano as a child, I did. Did I ever tell you that? Yes, could have been quite the professional, I'm sure, if I'd of stuck to it."

"But that tune," I persisted, "it's odd that it should be so familiar. Ah, well"—I sighed—"I suppose everyone at one time or another gets a tune stuck in their brain they can't put a name to. Yet it's strange—"

"I swear, Em!" she responded, throwing up her hands in frustration. "It's a flamin' wonder you don't investigate the disappearance of the sun every night. See a mystery in everything, you do!"

"Perhaps you're right." I chuckled. "Still, it's going to annoy me 'til I remember where I heard it."

"Aye, well, be that as it may, you'll have time enough to sort it all out tomorrow. Meanwhile," she added, giving the pillow one last thump, "you best be gettin' yourself ready for bed."

I waited until she had eased herself under the covers before announcing, "I'm afraid I won't be coming to bed, at least, not yet."

" 'Ere, now, wot's this you're sayin'?"

"As I never had time to investigate Lady St. Clair's bedroom this afternoon," I replied, dangling Hogarth's key ring right in front of her, "I thought I'd take the opportunity tonight."

"Searchin' her ladyship's room—why whatever for?" she asked, pushing herself up into a sitting position.

"I would have thought that was obvious. For answers."

She stifled a yawn. "Answers to what?"

"For one thing," I replied, noting her drowsiness with some trepidation, since I would later be in need of her services, "in finding out how our mysterious murderer arranged to leave the room so quickly and without being seen."

"And how do you intend to do that, eh?"

"That," I said, rising to a standing position,

"I don't know. But I'm bound and determined to try."

"I see," she answered with yet another yawn. "Well, you won't be needin' me then, will you?" she asked, easing herself down once more under the covers.

"Actually, I will," I replied, with just the slightest trace of a smile. "I need you to go on a journey."

That awakened her. "A journey! What now?" Violet eyed me warily. "What's this all about then, eh?"

"You've been telling me," I began, "of your out-of-body experiences. Well, now, Mrs. Violet Warner," I continued at a quickening pace before any objection on her part could be raised, "now's the time to put this astral ability of yours to good use."

"How'd you mean?"

"All I need is for you to 'flit off' as you put it, into Sir Charles and Lady Margaret's bedroom."

My request was met with a stunned silence before a torrent of protest rained down on me. "What! Their bedroom? Oh, Em, I couldn't! Why," she carried on, with a glance toward the mantel clock, "they're probably in there themselves, by this time."

"Actually, they are," I replied, calm of voice. "I heard them enter no more than five minutes ago."

"Ah, well," she announced, with a satisfied smile, whilst adjusting the covers around her, "there you are, you see. It wouldn't be proper, would it? And me, not even bein' dressed, like."

What was I to do with her?

"But, my dear Violet," was my exasperated reply, "they won't be able to see or hear you, will they?"

My one overriding complaint with my old friend was her inability to visualize the overall picture. I reminded her of the young woman found murdered only that morning and of her ladyship's funeral, but a few scant hours ago. I put it to her that with these macabre events still fresh in the minds of all parties concerned, it wouldn't take a Sherlock Holmes to realize what the topic of conversation would be when the opportunity arose for Sir Charles and Lady Margaret to speak in the privacy of their bedroom.

And, remembering snippets of talk heard round the dinner table, regarding both the colonel and the squire's penchant for engaging in an evening of cards before retiring, I was finally able to prevail upon Vi to pay a visit to the gaming room, as well as to the bedroom of the baronet and his wife.

Our "open-ear" policy we had adopted with respect to the St. Clairs' private conversation in the study had whetted my appetite for more. While realizing it was highly unlikely we would be so fortunate again, I therefore decided a more covert approach, utilizing my companion's astral ability, was the obvious answer.

I couldn't help but think how my two distinguished lodgers would have welcomed such spirited assistance on any number of cases they have been called upon to solve, notwithstanding Mr. H's aversion to matters dealing with, or pertaining to, the world of the supernatural.

As for myself, being but a mere mortal and unable to accompany my spiritualistic cohort on her ethereal wanderings, I nonetheless questioned her most extensively on her subsequent return. And, from my copious amount of notes made at that time, I am now able to set down in writing the following events as they occurred to my old and trusted friend.

She lay quite still upon the bed with palms down and arms extended on either side. With eyes closed, deep and rhythmic breathing followed until what she later described as a sensation of numbness, starting at the feet, spread upward over her entire body. She now experienced the effect of seeing through closed eyelids, the room illuminated by a pale but golden radiance. As the light slowly diminished, Violet Warner was left with a sense of residing in two bodies—one, physical, the other, fluidic.

It was at this point her spiritual self arose from the confines of its earthly shell as effortlessly as one would arise from a chair. With one last parting glance at her physical self lying in peaceful repose upon the bed, her ethereal self floated across the room and out to the hallway.

With the St. Clairs' bedroom being but a few steps from her own, she glided as silently as owl wings over to the door, hesitating for a moment or two before willing herself through, as if that solid-oak partition had never existed.

Once inside, Violet breathed a sigh of relief on finding the occupants of the room had not, as yet, taken to their bed.

"Oh, I do hope you'll excuse me for waltzin' in on the both of you like this," said she, feeling called upon to render an apology for what she considered was an unseemly astral intrusion on her part. "And even though I know you can't see or hear me," she carried on, "I feel that much better for the sayin' of it."

The matriarch of Haddley, attired in a lavender-laced nightgown, sat at her dressing table with her back to her husband. Her hair, freed from the upswept confines of the day, hung down about her shoulders in rich abundance. Staring resolutely into the mirror, she continued the brushing of it with sure and precise strokes.

The baronet, sans jacket and tie, lay sprawled on a chair with legs outstretched, while his hand aimlessly swished the remaining contents of his whiskey glass in a continuous circular motion. At intermittent intervals he cast disapproving glances toward his wife in the continuance of her nightly hair-brushing ritual.

"Margaret!" he at last cried out. "How much longer do you intend to thrash about like that with your hair!"

"Until I'm finished!" she snapped. "Ninety-seven, ninety-eight, ninety-nine, one hundred."

The brush was slammed down onto the veneered table top as Lady Margaret leaned slightly to her left in order that the reflected image of her husband be visible to her in the mirror. "If you paid as much attention to *your* personal habits, Charles, you'd be the better off for it," she snapped as thin delicate hands set about massaging both chin and neckline.

"Yes, well, fortunately my dear," replied her husband, setting his glass down and withdrawing his outstretched legs, "being chairman of a financial institution, with offices spread halfway round the Empire, doesn't require me to spend the better part of the night preparing for bed."

"Yes, it must keep you occupied, mustn't it? You spend more of your time in London than you do here at Haddley!"

"Can't say as I blame him," spoke Vi, to no one in particular.

"Not true, old darling. I came back earlier than intended from London only just last week."

"Yes! Believing I wouldn't be here!"

"But you *were* here, weren't you?" He bent over, and, pulling off both shoes, kicked them to one side. "With some story," he continued, once more leaning back in the chair, "about having words with your mother and leaving in a bit of a huff, as I recall you mentioning."

Turning back to her dressing table in agitation, she withdrew a silver case from the bottom drawer, extracted a cigarette, and lit it.

That was almost too much for Vi. " 'Ere, wot's this? A lady smoking a cigarette? Well, now, I've seen everything, I have!"

"It's true, Charles," she replied, as a halo of smoke ascended into the air. "Mother and I have never got along, though Lord knows I try."

Any acerbic response my old friend might have uttered was cut off by the lady of the manor suddenly asking, "And you?"

"I?" was her husband's bewildered response.

"Who else do you think I'm taking to?" she snapped.

"Well, not me, that's for flamin' sure," announced Vi, holding back a chuckle that would never have been heard in any event.

"Why did *you* return when you did, Charles?"

"No mystery, old darling," responded the baronet with a casual shrug of the shoulders. "As my business with Lord Harvey was concluded earlier than I had anticipated, I saw no reason to prolong my stay in London." He paused for a moment, studying the cigarette held airily in his wife's hand. "I wonder," he asked, biting his bottom lip in controlled annoyance, "if you'd be so kind as to put that thing out? I can well imagine what mother would have said if she saw you puffing away like some music hall tart."

"Good for you, Sir Charles!" cried Violet, with a soundless clap of her hands. "That's telling her!"

Quite unexpectedly, Lady Margaret submitted to his request by snubbing out the offending cigarette as she arose slowly from her chair.

"Well, we really don't have to worry anymore about what she would or wouldn't say, do we?" It was a rhetorical question, followed by another that demanded an answer. "Charles, there's something I have to know. Be truthful with me. You weren't involved in any way with her death, were you?"

"Ah-hah!" sang out Vi. "Now we're gettin' somewhere!"

"*Involved*! Good Lord, Margaret! What on earth are you talking about?"

"Oh, Charles, really! You must have noticed the scratches on her throat as if she had been engaged in some sort of struggle."

"Well *I* didn't!" exclaimed my old friend.

"And that sickly odor hanging over her bed," continued his wife, "couple that with the Warner woman babbling on about someone being in the room, and—"

"Babbling!"

It was now the baronet's turn to rise from his chair. "Oh, I see. That's it, is it? You believe I'm responsible for mother's demise, do you? And perhaps I also bashed in the head of that poor creature of a girl wandering about the grounds? Don't be daft!"

Lady Margaret started to speak.

"No! Let me finish!" her husband exclaimed, picking up his coat, which lay hanging off the edge of the bed. "If you remember my telling you, old darling," he continued, while fishing around the pockets, presumably for a cigarette, "I was down in the library when I first heard the commotion from Mother's bedchamber."

Cigaretteless, he flung the coat back on the bed, and crossing over to his wife's dressing table, withdrew one from the silver case, and lit it.

"I will admit," he went on, as two thin streams of smoke escaped from his nostrils, "that I did sense her death had not been as peaceful as it was purported to have been."

Lady Margaret moved to the edge of the bed and sat down, her eyes never leaving her husband. "Yet you said nothing. Why?"

"As much as I hate to say this, old thing, I thought you were somehow responsible."

"My very words to Em!" proclaimed my companion, triumphantly, even though she was, at this point, becoming frustrated in her attempt to enter into the conversation.

"I?" An astonished gasp from Lady M. "Why would I—?"

"No one likes being second in command," her husband interjected. "With mother gone you could at last take your rightful place as lady of the manor." Then with a knowing smile, he added, "No more having to bow to her every demand or even having to sneak off for a cigarette, eh, Margaret? The thing of it is," he continued, "I suspected my 'lady-in waiting' simply got tired of waiting. How you must have hated her dominance over you."

His wife sprang from the bed, her eyes flashing. "I don't deny that her ladyship and I were never close! But what would have been the point of . . ."

The word murder was left unspoken.

"If I've had to endure her presence all this time," she began again, "what would a few more months, or a year, at best, have mattered? She was, after all, an old woman."

"And you, an impatient one!"

"So, you actually believe I was the one who—"

"Why not?" he quickly responded. "You think *me* guilty. Though for whatever reason, I haven't the foggiest."

Astral eyes continued to dart back and forth between husband and wife.

"Haven't the foggiest, you say! Oh, Charles," she replied, with a hollow laugh, "don't take me for a fool. I'm well aware our financial situation is not all that it should be. And, with at least half of your mother's estate going to you on her death—well, what am I to think?"

Sir Charles threw his head back in good-natured laughter.

Both women eyed him curiously.

"I'm sorry, darling," he said at last, when his laughter had subsided. "But don't you see the irony of it all? You, thinking me guilty of matricide, said nothing in order to protect me. I, in thinking it was you, did the same."

"Oh, *I* see," spoke Violet, in her typical caustic fashion, "it were out of love for each other, were it? Don't make me laugh. Protectin' each other for your own interest, be more like it."

"Then, I suppose we really do care about each other, Charlie." A small smile played lovingly about her lips as she spoke.

"Well, of course we do, Maggie, old darling."

" 'Ere! Charlie and Maggie now, is it? Well, if they're gettin' into *that*, I'd best be gone!" And with one last look at the two of them, she added, "And in any event, I don't know if I believe a bleedin' word I heard here tonight from either one of you!"

Propelling herself along as if riding on a cushion of air, she headed straight for the door after making one small turn to pass directly through the body of Lady Margaret. In that instant, an unearthly chill swept over the baronet's wife as her entire body gave way to an involuntary shudder.

Violet Warner, harboring a satisfied smile, was on her way to the gaming room.

Seeing the colonel sitting hunched over the card table with a look of utter despair on that jowly face, it was clear to Vi that Dame Fortune had bypassed him in favor of the younger St. Clair.

"Another game lost!" thundered the old man through that all-encircling moustache, while slamming down his cards and in the process nearly upsetting the glasses set before them.

The squire's attitude to all this was one of mild amusement, coupled with an unconcerned shrug of his shoulders.

"You're under no obligation to play, old boy."

"I don't need you to tell me what my obligations are!" was the bellowing response, delivered in true militaristic fashion. "If you had served in Her Majesty's forces as I, you'd know a sense of duty and obligation are the prime requisites for an officer and a gentleman. By gad, indeed you would, sir!"

"And what of honor, Colonel?" asked the squire as he set about gathering up the cards. "Doesn't honor require an officer and a gentleman to pay for any losses he may accrue— say, at cards, for instance?"

"You'll be paid! You'll be paid every penny, I assure you!" thundered the old soldier as his muttonlike hand rummaged through an inside pocket before at last extracting a cigar.

"You're not lighting up one of *those* now, are you!" wailed Violet. "Why, I'd as soon as smell a rubber boot, I would," she added, while failing in her attempt to wave away the offending aroma with a hand more vaporous than the object of her annoyance.

"Yes, yes, I'm sure I'll be paid, my dear Colonel. But since a good three weeks have elapsed since last I saw the color of your money, the question remains, when? And while I admit," he continued, in a casual offhanded manner, "to having lost more than the hundred quid you owe me at the tables in London on a single evening, the amount for a man in your position would be—well, you see what I mean."

Visibly shaken, the response from the colonel was nonetheless delivered in measured tones. "I have told you, Squire, you shall have your money. Before month's end, if you wish to put a time on it."

"Before month's—ah, I see." A knowing smile from his opponent. "I take it you're thinking ahead to the reading of her ladyship's will. If so, I wouldn't bank too heavily on that, old boy."

Blotches of red appeared on two fleshy cheeks. "That will do sir! This evening is at an end!"

Flinging out his words as if dressing down an orderly, the old soldier pushed himself back from the table and, attempting to rise, found to his chagrin that his portly frame was unable to extricate itself from the chair with any degree of ease.

The squire, in an effort to cover the embarrassment of the moment, bade him stay with the offer of a replenishment to his drink.

Eyeing the extended decanter, as would a child a jar of candy, there was only the briefest hesitation before that massive bulk was once more firmly entrenched in the chair.

"Aye, that's right," breathed Vi, with a sigh of relief. "We can't have you leavin' yet. Why, I haven't heard enough from either one of you to fill a bird's ear."

"I only mention a probable loss to you in finding a pot of gold at the end of the will due to what you may have heard described in the family as 'the incident.' "

"Incident? What incident? No idea what you're talking about, old boy."

"Ah, St. Innocent, himself!" was the mocking response from the squire. Then in angry condemnation, he added, "Good Lord, man! You put a bullet through my father's head and have the nerve to sit there and ask me, what incident?" He shook his head in disbelief.

"You're a wonder, my dear Colonel. You are indeed."

"Wot's this you're sayin', now?" sang out Violet. "That old Colonel Windbag here actually shot his lordship?" Both arms were flung upward in a gesture of futility. "I dunno." She sighed. "Seems like everyone in this ruddy household is hiding more skeletons in their closet than a ruddy graveyard!"

"If you're referring to that unfortunate hunting accident of a few years back," the old man coolly responded, "that's all that it was—a hunting accident."

"Was it, indeed? Yes, mistook my father for a stag, as I remember your saying," was the sarcastic rejoinder.

"Then perhaps you'll also remember," snapped the colonel from behind a cloud of billowing blue smoke, "it was I who saved his lordship's life during the Punjab campaign! And for that—"

"And for that," echoed the younger man, "my father gave you free bed and board at Haddley for the remainder of your life. Yes, I've heard it all before. But that wasn't enough, was it? Over the years it must have occurred to you, were his lordship out of the way, a marriage between you and her ladyship was not without its possibilities. Ergo—the hunting 'accident.' Am I right or am I not, Colonel?"

"By gad, sir, that's quite an imagination you have! You've missed your calling—indeed you have, sir. A writer for the penny dreadfuls, that's your ticket!"

"But her ladyship turned you down, didn't she, old boy?" pressed the squire, ignoring the colonel's barbed remarks.

The elderly officer eyed him coldly. "She spoke to you of this?"

"Not in so many words. But I knew. We all did. You see, what you failed to realize, while playing the role of the lovesick swain, was that mother never believed, in her heart of hearts, the shooting had been an accident. Still, she held true to his lordship's wishes that you remain here, while you, taking advantage of the situation, continued to press for her hand in wedlock. True enough?"

A moment of silence followed. "It's true," the colonel spoke at last, "that I've always thought of your mother as a very handsome woman, and, I daresay, there might have been, over the years, one or two occasions when I—"

"Over the years! My dear chap, you should know as well as I nothing is sacred or secret at Haddley. Your last offer of a life of connubial bliss took place no less than a week ago. Rumor has it that mother not only rejected you but suggested it would now be best if you were to look for accommodation elsewhere."

"Rumor!" snorted the old soldier. "That's all that it is—rumor! And you'll oblige me with an apology. And that, sir, is an order!"

"You're not in the military now, Wyndgate! And I'm not one of your subordinates!"

According to Vi, words were hurled across

the table as the squire rose angrily to his feet.

"I wish to God you were, sir!" boomed the colonel. "The army has a way of dealing with insolence!"

" 'Ere, simmer down, the both of you!" demanded an unseen third party.

As if on cue there followed an awkward silence from both gentlemen with the squire at last resuming his seat.

I remember Violet telling me how pleased she was with herself, attributing her part in the easing of the situation to ethereal suggestion.

"Asked me to leave, did she? Do you have any proof of what you say?" growled the old man. "No," he added, without waiting for a reply, "I thought not. By the great Lord Harry, perhaps you also think me guilty of having done the old girl in as well!"

"I thought that was obvious," remarked the squire.

"Aha! So, it were the old boy—I knew it!" cried my old friend, conveniently forgetting that her original suspicion lay with Lady Margaret.

"Let's face it, Colonel, if her ladyship were alive today, you'd be out walking the streets or knocking at the door of the old soldiers' home—or wherever it is old soldiers go. Come on, man," he taunted, "fess up. They say it's good for the soul."

Plump sausagelike fingers angrily squashed the cigar stub into the tray, as that massive head jutted forward to meet his accuser, eye to eye. "You, St. Clair," he thundered, "are a bloody fool!"

"Then again," thought Violet, thoroughly intimidated by this sudden outburst, "maybe it weren't him, after all."

"To even suggest," railed the old man, "that I had anything to do with her ladyship's death is absurd. Chloroform, indeed! Shell and saber are the tools of my profession, sir."

"I said nothing of chloroform, Colonel."

"What! What!" Fumbling for words, the old gentleman quickly regained ground by asserting, "I simply assumed the odor was apparent to everyone present within her ladyship's bedroom, the chemical being not unknown to me from time spent in army hospitals. You, sir, I'm sure, are as well informed as I with the chemical."

"Oh, come now, old boy," laughed the younger man, "why on earth would I . . ."

"Money, sir! Money is the cause of more murders than ever it was with affairs of the heart."

"And what's that supposed to mean?"

For the first time since entering the room, Violet saw a slight trace of a smile hiding 'neath that flowing moustache.

"I shall be happy to explain, my dear sir."

The old army colonel was now on the offensive.

Having gained the squire's and Vi's undivided attention, he continued to savor the moment by proceeding, very slowly, to light up yet another cigar, much to my companion's annoyance.

"You mentioned earlier," he began, through small puffs of smoke, "that you have, on occasion, lost more than *my* accumulated debt in a single evening, what?"

A slight nod from the squire was accompanied by an amused if not a somewhat circumspect smile.

"And I believe you, sir. I truly do," continued the old colonel, on receiving the silent but wary affirmation. "In fact," he added, leaning his bulk forward whilst fixing an accusatory eye on the man opposite, "your losses now total well into the thousands, true or not, my dear Squire?"

St. Clair shifted uncomfortably in his chair while a forced laugh followed his derisive reply. "Thousands! Oh, come now, Colonel. I believe *you're* the one who should turn his hand to the writing of fiction."

The old soldier, passing on the remark, casually rolled his cigar twixt thumb and forefinger, seemingly absorbed in the smoke lazily wafting its way upward before responding. "It's easy enough to take an old man for his money, but it's a different story with the lads in London, is it not, young sir?"

"I'm afraid, Wyndgate, old chap, I haven't the slightest idea what you're talking about."

"George Bascombe. Nigel Royce-Smythe."

The names, casually injected, achieved the effect the old man most certainly knew they would.

Vi reported watching St. Clair's fingers tighten their grip on his glass in an effort to still a shaking hand. "How do you know of these men?'' he asked in a voice no more than a whisper.

"I'm not the fool you take me for, Squire. I'm well aware both gentlemen own two of the most select and private gaming rooms in London's West End and that each has barred you from entering pending payment of your debts. Which no doubt," he went on, "explains your unexpected return. Being expelled from your favorite haunts, you had no alternative but to return to Haddley, what?''

Having shot this verbal cannonball of information across the table, the old man eased himself into a self-satisfied smile, and, leaning back, rested those massive hands on that considerable paunch of his to await the outcome of its impact.

"What the devil is all this?'' the squire angrily retorted. "Who gave you permission to pry into my private life?''

The words were flung out so suddenly and with such force that, according to Vi, "I almost evaporated in fright, I did!''

"It was her ladyship actually,'' replied the colonel in a calm manner.

"Mother! That is to say, her ladyship had you . . . I don't believe it—not a word!''

"True enough, in any event, young sir. It seemed that her suspicions were aroused when she discovered a pair of gold candlesticks missing from the salon. Then, as I recall, it was a set of seventeenth-century gold serving plates and so on, and so on.''

Vi was aghast. "Robbin' the place blind,

were you? Why Squire, I am disappointed," she clucked, disapprovingly, while airily drifting in to occupy an unattended chair at the table. "Never would have thought it of you, I wouldn't."

Cigar ashes were casually flicked into the tray by the old soldier as he continued on, unperturbed by the younger man's agitation. "Knowing of your compulsion for cards, plus the fact that no less than three months ago her ladyship told you no more money would be forthcoming to pay off your continual losses, it didn't take the old girl too long to put two and two together. At which point, she saw fit to take me into her confidence. I was asked to make certain inquiries, which I did, by corresponding with an acquaintance of mine in London. He in turn hired an operative whose detailed account of your activities was forwarded to me, thence to her ladyship. Shall I go on?"

" 'Ere, not so fast, me old duck," sang out Vi. "I've got to remember all this for Em, I have."

There was no immediate response from the squire, who sat in brooding silence.

"I say, old boy," the colonel added in jocular admonishment, "if you had to sneak about selling off the house in piecemeal fashion, so to speak, you shouldn't have been so obvious. I understand the upper level of this august household holds a veritable treasure trove of objets d'art, as they say."

Henry St. Clair rose slowly to his feet and

began quietly pacing the floor, pausing only to spew out his reply. "Half of what's here will be mine someday, anyway—so, even if what you're saying is true, what of it?"

"Ah," he replied with a wagging of a chubby finger, "but someday is already here, isn't it? That's my point, old boy. With her ladyship gone to her just reward, I imagine your line of credit would now stretch into infinity."

The squire returned to his chair, and, pulling it back, sat sideways to the table with legs outstretched on a small leather ottoman. "So, what you're saying is, I murdered my mother for the inheritance to pay off my gambling debts and continue in my wicked, wicked ways, is that it? Then tell me, Colonel, why is it you made no mention of this to the police? Or the fact that you smelled chloroform? You had ample opportunity this morning."

The questions were followed by much huffing and puffing from the other side of the table.

"Then let *me* tell *you*!" The squire swung round to face the old soldier head on. "First, because you know the accusation is completely false. Second, and more importantly, at least from your standpoint, you realized accusing me would result in brother Charles seeing to it your role as Haddley's perpetual guest would be brought to an end. Blood being thicker than water—that sort of thing. What?" he added, mockingly.

"You had the same opportunity as I to voice your opinions to the police," announced the older man. "Yet you remained silent as well—why?"

"In truth, old boy," announced the source in an offhanded manner, "Haddley doesn't need the scandal. Whatever status we have left in the village would be completely destroyed—not to mention what would happen if the London papers got hold of it. I simply thought it best to keep the status quo."

"Whatever your reasons, Squire, you are quite wrong about my part in all this. As perhaps," he imparted thoughtfully, "I am of you."

"In any event," replied the younger man, "what's done is done."

"But, look here, St. Clair, that young snip of a girl they found this morning—could be a bit sticky for the family, what?"

"I shouldn't think so," answered the squire, rising from the chair whilst patting his mouth to stifle a yawn. "From what I can make of it all, it was one of the local girls done in by one of the lads from the stable. I've told the inspector as much. I doubt that Twillings will hold the family responsible for any sordid affair involving the help."

Alas, at this point, my companion found she could no longer continue her astral visitation, for she was now aware of impatient tugs from some invisible cord within her ethereal form pulling her back—while at the same time experiencing sharp, tiny points of pain to the forehead of her physical body. As this was the first time Violet had strayed for such a prolonged period, she became quite frightened.

According to Violet, on willing herself back she experienced a great whooshing of wind that swept her along through a black and limitless tunnel before arriving back once more safe and sound within the comfort of her bed.

TWELVE

A Riddle Solved

〜WHILE VI WAS busily engaged in her ethereal eavesdropping, I had taken the opportunity of investigating the bedroom of the late Lady St. Clair.

And what a dismal room it was from what I could see of it by the small glow of the lamp Hogarth had so very generously provided me.

I had thought it prudent to keep the flame turned only so high, for I had noticed before entering that a good quarter-inch gap separated door from floor, and I wanted no telltale sign of a flickering light escaping into the outside hall. I feared, should my presence be discovered, the least that could happen would be an abrupt termination of my stay at Haddley. The worst, my untimely demise at the hands of, as the police would say, a person or persons unknown. Later events would prove I was being neither morbid nor overly dramatic.

I swung my lamp to the right to find four posters standing, I thought, ominously on

145

guard at each corner of a velvet-draped Elizabethan bed, the sight of which left me with an uneasy feeling as I recalled my companion's tale of the old woman struggling for her life upon that very bed.

A turn to the wall opposite revealed a grandiose, large-as-life family portrait which I took to be that of the St. Clairs, and done a good many years ago by the look of two small boys staring wistfully up into the eyes of their parents. I noted the placement of the painting in relationship to the bed and concluded it had been hung in that particular location so her ladyship might lie and gaze across the room, and yes, I suppose, across the years, at a family whose existence was now limited to the bordered confines of a gilded frame.

On a personal note, I'm afraid I was not all that impressed with the painting, the figures being too stiff and formal for my liking and the waxlike tonal quality to the skin left me completely unimpressed with the work. However, I reminded myself, I was not here as an art critic, but as a detective.

Where to begin?

I took it upon myself to play the role of the murderer. Leaning over the now empty bed, I imagined myself being engaged in that most heinous deed. Violet would now be outside demanding entrance. My first instinct was to rush to the window. I did so. Pushing back the curtains and undoing the latch, I leaned out to discover it would be a formidable drop indeed to the pavement below, with walls too smooth for a climb in either direction.

A secret panel? Perhaps. If so, it would not have been the first of such stately homes in England to have undisclosed exits installed as a hasty retreat from the king's soldiers or Cromwellian Roundheads, depending on one's politics. Or even for the purposes of quickly taking leave of a bed due to the unexpected late-night arrival of either master or mistress, depending on one's sex.

As it was, I spent a good fifteen minutes carefully making my way round the room, quietly thumping each section of the paneled walls in the hope of hearing a hollowness of sound from within. Alas, I confess my efforts were to no avail. Violet, I told myself, might be able to disappear into thin air, but I doubted if our murderer was capable of mastering the feat.

I thought perhaps a trap door might be the answer but quickly discarded the idea. A rug of oriental design covered almost the entire floor area. It would have been impossible for someone to pull back a portion of it, drop down to the floor below, and have left the rug in its original position.

It seemed I would have to resign myself to having failed in solving the riddle unless I discounted my companion's version of the night in question.

This I would never do.

No, there had to be something I had overlooked. But what?

While pondering on this, a brief sparkle of light caught the corner of my eye. I turned, questioningly, holding the lamp out before me. Gone! No, there it was again. The lamp, when held at just the right angle was causing a reflected shimmer from—ah, there, the area between bed and night table. I squeezed an arm down and extracted the item in question. In bringing it closer to the light, words cannot express my utter astonishment in finding it to be—the missing earring!

I held it in the palm of my hand, studying it carefully, scarcely believing my eyes. The missing earring of half-moon design, the mate to that worn by the murdered girl, found here! I noted a defective clasp as being the probable cause of its presence, with the owner, in all likelihood, being totally unaware of her loss. Lowering myself down upon that great bed, I continued to stare at my find as a thousand and one questions raced through my mind.

Had her ladyship known the girl had been quartered in the upstairs room? Had she been here before or after the old woman's murder? Or was the young girl herself culpable of the deed? No, I reasoned, that at least could be ruled out. From Violet's description of the attacker, it had not been someone of the girl's size and stature with whom my old companion had grappled in her vigorous but one-sided translucent encounter.

Although the earring irrefutably confirmed that a link existed between the two murdered women, I was unable to grasp, as yet, the significance of that link. If I but knew the identity of the young woman found dead among the leaves of autumn . . .

"Solve that, m'girl," I wearily told myself, "and no doubt all the pieces will start falling prettily into place."

Although pleased in the finding of the ear-ring, I was less than satisfied in my attempt to unravel the riddle of the disappearing mur-derer. Slipping the earring into my purse, I consoled myself with the hope Violet had been fortunate enough to wander into ongoing con-versations of a more revealing nature. Thus it was with mixed feelings I decided to with-draw from the scene.

Turning toward the door, I was stopped by my own fear and bewilderment as I watched an inanimate doorknob begin to revolve slowly on its own! Gathering my wits about me, I extinguished the lamp and quickly pressed myself up against the wall on the op-posite side of the door frame. And there I stood, with heart a-pounding, while the door very slowly was eased open.

From my position I had the advantage of not being seen but the disadvantage of not knowing the intruder's identity. He did not enter directly into the room itself, but stood just inside the open doorway. I say *he* for I now remembered hearing a heaviness of feet to floor in the hallway but moments before. Believing it to be a servant I had thought little of it until now.

What to do?

As I certainly had no intention of confront-ing the man, I waited until at last I was able to afford myself a grateful sigh of relief as he quietly departed, closing the door from be-hind.

It was to be a short-lived respite.

As if having second thoughts, he reentered, this time leaving the door slightly ajar so that a smattering of light from the outside hall eliminated, to some small extent, the opaque-ness from within. And while the niceties of so-ciety deem the act of perspiring unladylike, I must confess I stood bathed in an all-enveloping sweat as my auditory senses, heightened by fear to the nth degree, picked up the sound of heavy breathing, advancing through the blackness toward me.

A slight whoosh of air cut through the still-ness as a hand shot out, grazing the bottom of my chin. The absence of light had obviously resulted in a miscalculation of his aim, for the hand slid down in a tightening grip round my throat.

He intended to strangle me!

I remember making odd gurgling sounds and beginning to grow faint as more and more pressure was applied to my windpipe.

Do something, Emma! I screamed inwardly.

If I was about to die, it would not be with-out a struggle. Lifting my foot as high as I could, I brought it down with all the force I could muster on the toe of his shoe. There was a groan as his fingers relaxed their grip, albeit for a second. I took that second to gulp in air. As I hadn't the strength to pull his hands from my throat, I made one last desperate attempt to claw my assailant's face. But, held at arm's length, my hands did nothing but thrash about the darkness, with nails that flayed naught but air. Then, in a semiconscious state, I slumped to the floor.

And then the strangest thing happened.

As I lay there, I saw myself as a little girl sitting under the apple tree in the backyard of my parents' home. I looked up to see my mother coming out onto the back stoop. She stood there, drying her hands on her apron and, on calling out to me, asked if I had eaten any of the apples.

"No Mama," I lied. "Why?"

Her answer was that they were far too green and then, overemphasizing her concern, added if I ate them I would get very sick and die. Satisfied she had instilled in me the worst possible fear with respect to an overindulgence of apple eating, she turned and went back inside. As the screen door slammed shut behind her, I let out a moan.

"Oh," I wailed, "I'm going to die! I'm going to die!"

It was a phrase I found myself repeating over and over as I lay sprawled on the floor drifting in and out of consciousness, dimly aware of a slight pressure on my wrist being made by a forefinger and thumb. My assailant, whose heavy breathing I found myself listening to with an odd sense of detachment, was bending over me in what seemed to me at the time, an attempt to take my pulse. To see, I presume, if I had finally passed through the final veil.

In truth, I thought I had.

Through flickering eyelids, I now saw a blue

phosphorous light outlined in the shape of a human form, standing no more than a foot away from me! I continued staring at it, more in fascination than fear, as its unearthly glow continued to pulsate every few seconds in varying degrees of intensity. My first impression was this light was the spirit form of my mother, who had come to take me over to that other side, a thought I quickly discarded when my assailant suddenly let out a gasp.

He had seen it, too!

The last thing I remember was my would-be murderer quickly taking his leave. After that, all else was a complete void.

Whoever or whatever it was, the apparition had saved my life.

"Feelin' better now then, are you, luv?"

I shook my head as, with blurry eyes, I tried, with a modicum of success, to focus in on the figure standing over me.

It was only when I made a half-hearted attempt to rise that I realized I was in a bed.

Vi's bed. Back in her bedroom. But how?

Jumbled images spun round in my brain. A brain that was desperately trying to remember, in chronological order, missing segments of time.

"Now that you're back in the land of the living, I've a nice hot cup of tea for you, if you've a mind for it."

I had, indeed.

It is my belief that tea, notwithstanding its flavor, has within it certain medicinal properties for the clearing of heads, the curing of colds and, in general, an elixir for all manner of minor aches and pains. It is also my contention we British are what we are today because of it and, I've no doubt, should this sceptered isle ever be deprived of its national drink, the Empire would come crumbling down in disarray within a fortnight.

I consumed the tea and was well into my second cup before the questions came pouring out. "How did I get here? Who found me? What time is it?"

"Why it's quarter past ten," she answered with a smile.

"Ten! Why, it must be later than that. It was well after nine when I went down the hall to her ladyship's bedroom."

"Em!" she exclaimed. "That were last night. It's ten, ten in the morning."

"You mean I've slept—?"

"Aye. And after what you've been through, I'd say you deserved every minute of it."

What I've been through? It was only then that I recalled fingers tightening round my throat and the specter of the spirit who had saved me.

"Vi," I said, very seriously, as I handed her my now empty cup, "I've every reason to believe Haddley is haunted."

"Haunted!" Her trembling hand tried unsuccessfully to still her cup, which rattled precariously in its saucer. "Why, what ever would make you say such a thing as that?" She asked, replacing cup to table.

I related the events of my near death and of the spirit whose appearance on the scene was the reason for my being alive today to tell the tale. When I had finished, I had expected her reaction to be either one of horror or astonishment but never one of disbelief. I had accepted her astral abilities in good faith, but after relating *my* encounter with the supernatural her reaction was little more than a childish giggle.

"Really, Violet!" I exploded. "If I'm not to be taken seriously, perhaps it's best I return to London!"

"Seriously, she says! Why, of course I takes you seriously. Why shouldn't I?"

"I don't understand, first you—"

"Blue in color, were it?"

I was beginning to get a headache.

"I think," said I, with a gentle rubbing of hand to forehead, "somewhere along the way we've managed to sail right past each other."

"Why, I can explain it all, I can," she assured me, drawing a chair alongside the bed. "After being whisked back from the gaming room, the first thing I see is me body lyin' quiet-like in bed, but no Emma. Well, now, I says to meself, that's queer, that is. I figured you'd be back here by that time. That's when I gets this funny feelin' that summat's wrong. So, even though I was still feelin' woozy-like, I forced meself to stay out of body long enough to make it down to her ladyship's bedroom. And it were like seein' a repeat of the last time I were there. Only now, it were you! Strugglin' for your very life, you was. Thinkin' fast, I figured if I could somehow make meself visible, he'd think he had an extra body, so to speak, to contend with. I've never done such a thing before, nor did I ever want to, come to think of it, but anything was worth a try. 'Willpower,' as old Bessie would say. 'Willpower, that's the ticket!' So, I held me breath and concentrated for as long and as hard as I could."

"You stood there holding your breath?" I asked incredulously.

"Aye. It helps me concentration. But it didn't work, I couldn't materialize, leastways not in the way I hoped."

"So my mysterious blue-spirit from the great beyond turns out to be none other than Violet Warner!" I chortled. It was the first time in days I had had a good laugh. "Never mind, you did well enough, old girl!" I cried out in delight. "Well enough, indeed! By managing to appear, if only in outline form, surrounded by your aura of light, you saved my life! My dear, wonderful, Mrs. Warner," I smiled, through tears of gratitude, "you're a treasure, you are!"

"Well," she replied, with a good natured if somewhat embarrassed laugh, "it's about flippin' time someone noticed."

"But did you, in any way," I asked, "see who it was that attacked me?"

"No." She sighed. "Well, I was too worried about you, weren't I? I mean, what with you lyin' there, and all."

"I only wish *I* had. But, as you say, in the darkness and the state of mind we were both in at the time, it's understandable. But how did I get back here?"

"It were just like before. I flits off back to me room and then after slippin' into me body as nice as you please, I high-tails it back to her ladyship's bedchamber. You don't remember me helpin' you up or walkin' you back down the hall?"

"Only vaguely," I admitted, "now that you mention it."

"Never you worry, luv. It'll all come back, like as not."

I now pressed her to tell what, if anything, she had heard with respect to her astral wanderings. When she had finished I found it hard to contain my elation. Not only had she proved herself, and more, but the information gathered by Violet now gave me a clearer perspective as to the overall picture. As for my companion, she was not at all sure much had been accomplished.

"Weren't no big mystery after all why they returned to Haddley when they did," she said. "Their reasons seemed innocent enough."

"Hmmm," I answered.

" 'Course," she went on, "we now have a motive for each of 'em wantin' her ladyship done away with. S'pose that's summat, at least."

"Yes," I concurred. "Lady Margaret's dislike of her ladyship and wanting control over the affairs of Haddley should not be so lightly discounted."

"And Sir Charles," added Vi, "sufferin' like he is from a financial loss, and the squire from gamblin' debts."

"Not to mention," I said, "Colonel Wyndgate. *If* what the squire said is true, it could be a death blow for someone his age to be turned out onto the streets. And it's easy enough to see their point in the disastrous effect a murder, or even the suspicion of one, could have on the family as a whole, should all this be brought to light in a court of law."

"Aye. True enough, I suppose. But, are we any the better off for the knowin' of it?"

"We're building," I replied, "inch by inch. We now know their motives for murder and their reason for keeping it quiet when it occurred. And in any event," I added, bringing my hand up and lightly stroking my throat, "we can take some sort of pyrrhic pride in the knowledge there's one person who believes we know much more than we do."

"Oooh, look at that!" Vi cried out. "Still see red welt marks on your neck, I can. I think it's high time we took ourselves out of here before your Mr. Holmes has to investigate *our* murder!"

"The situation *is* becoming quite dicey," I admitted. "But I've much to do."

"Like what?"

"See Inspector Thackeray, for one thing. He'll want to have the statue examined. That alone should bring him around to our way of thinking, as should the earring—Good Lord, the earring! My purse, Vi, where's my purse?"

" 'Ere, don't go gettin' yourself all in a dither, it's right here where I put it beside the bed," she answered, picking it up and handing it to me. "And what's all this about an earring, eh?"

In lieu of an answer, I rummaged frantically through the contents. After a worried moment or two I at last found it. Bringing it forth, I held it out for her inspection.

"And very nice it is too, I'm sure," said Vi, eyeing the earring of half-moon design. "But I doubt whether I'd be all that upset if I had lost it."

"You don't understand," I replied. "It isn't mine. It belongs to the dead girl. I found it in Lady St. Clair's bedroom."

"Her ladyship's bedroom! Why, whatever was it doing there?"

"At this point, I'm sorry to say, I don't know," I answered, slowly turning the earring over in my hand.

She clucked her tongue in sympathy as I set about relating my adventures from the night before, including the moment when I stood watching the door being opened.

"Would've jumped out of me skin, I would 'ave," she shuddered.

"Well," I replied, with a chuckle, "I did something a little less physical than that."

"What, then?"

"I simply hid behind the—"

I stopped in mid-sentence and stared vacantly into space as my mind continued to race along with the speed of a whippet.

"Why, whatever is wrong with you, Em?"

"Oh, Vi," I replied, casting aside the covers and easing myself out of bed. "I've been such a fool!"

"Emma Hudson!" demanded my old friend. "You get yourself back into bed this very minute. You're in no shape to—"

"No, no, I'm quite all right," I answered.

Too excited to take a chair, I began to pace the floor before whirling round to face my companion.

"The bedchamber was never locked, was it? No," I answered for her. "A fact known to every member of the household, family and servant alike. The murderer," I continued, at a now quickening pace, "taking advantage of that, quietly entered the room and, after locking it from within, set about the task of administering the chloroform. It was while her ladyship was struggling vainly for her life that you floated in."

Vi said nothing but sat bobbing her head in agreement.

"In astral form," I continued, "you could do nothing but return to your bedroom, which you did. The deed now done, it was time for our mysterious friend to take leave of the room. But by now, you were outside the door with Hogarth, demanding entrance. The murderer had but one choice—to hide."

"I'll grant you that much," spoke Vi. "But where? That's my question."

"Why," I answered, with a self-satisfied smile, "the same place I did. Behind the door."

"Behind the—!"

"Exactly! When the master key was inserted in the lock by Hogarth, in you came."

"Aye."

"In came Hogarth."

"Aye."

"And in came the St. Clairs accompanied by Dr. Morley and the colonel. At least," I said,

pausing for breath, "that's what you believed."

"But that's the way it happened!" exclaimed
Violet.

"Not quite, I'm afraid, my dear Mrs. Warner. All but one of those assembled had entered the room. In the confusion of the
moment, our calculating culprit had but to
step out from behind the door to mingle, quite
innocently, with the others. And who was any
the wiser?"

I shook my head at the simplicity of it all.
Secret panels and trap doors, indeed! In my
haste to uncover some elaborate and/or ingen-
ious plan of escape, I had committed the investigative sin of overlooking the obvious.

This admission on my part took me back to
a time when, as a little girl, my father would
astonish me in sleight-of-hand magic with a
deck of playing cards. How I would beg,
plead, and cajole him for the secret behind the
trick. And when at last I was rewarded with
the answer, I would be the most disappointed
of children.

"But, Papa," I would wail, "there must be
more to it than that. It's too easy!"

Then that handsome head of his would be
thrown back in laughter.

"Never overlook the obvious, Emma," he
would say. "Never overlook the obvious."

I'm afraid I did, Papa. At least, for a while.

THIRTEEN

Goodbye, My Sailor Boy

AFTER DRESSING, WE headed downstairs to privately partake in a late lunch consisting of soup, buttered scones, tea, and the most delicious of minced tarts. Feeling the better for it, I was now ready to set off for Twillings.

As some sort of transport was needed for my journey, Vi escorted me out to the stables, where a mountain of a man with a face as leathery as the apron he wore was busily engaged in the shoeing of a horse.

"Mrs. Warner," he said, eyeing our approach. "Been a while since you was out here."

"This 'ere's Mrs. Hudson, Ben. She'd like to go into the village. We was wonderin' if there was anything available, like."

He stood up, nodding to me, while thoughtfully stroking his hand over a bristled chin. "Don't know who'd be available to take you, missus. Bit short-handed, you see. What with one of the lads not showing up, and all."

161

"That would be Will," I said, before silently reproaching myself for the saying of it.

"How'd you know that, then?"

"He's at the village," I replied indirectly, in the hope he'd leave it at that.

"That so? Not mixed up in any way with that dead girl he came across, is he?"

"Why do you ask?" I hedged.

"Heard talk, same as others."

As I had neither the time nor the wish to engage the man in an ongoing conversation with respect to what we knew, I simply stated one of the reasons for my going to the village was to return with the lad himself. At that point, I tactfully changed the subject by asking Ben what he had available for my journey to Twillings, and was informed that the best he could offer in the way of transportation would be a small cart.

"Driven before, have you?" he asked.

"Not that often," I confessed.

"Ah, well, then, you'll be wantin' Daisy."

"Daisy?"

"A gentle a mare as ever there was, missus, and no mistake. Knows her way there and back, does our Daisy."

And so it was, with wagon hitched, earring in purse, marble statue packaged, tied, and placed in back, I readied myself behind the reins.

"You're sure now, you don't want me comin' along?" asked Vi.

"No, as I say, it's best you stay behind to keep an eye on anything out of the ordinary that may occur."

"Like another murder or two?" she asked, only half-jokingly.

"Heaven forbid!"

The ride to Twillings, though slow, was at least uneventful. The mare, a docile creature, set her own speed and no amount of cajolery on my part could change that steady, plodding pace. I was beginning to wonder when, or if, I would ever reach my destination. I'm quite sure, had I been but a few years younger, I could have walked the distance in half the time. But, arrive I did and, on asking directions from one of the locals, found the station with little or no trouble at all.

"Mrs. Hudson, 'pon my word!" exclaimed the inspector, as I made my entrance. "This is a surprise. Please, come in."

I entered a windowless office with walls of dull brown and took a chair in front of a desk strewn with the obligatory necessities—ink, pen, ledgers, sheafs of papers, pipe, and tray—plus a newspaper, opened at a half-completed crossword puzzle.

"I am quite busy, you understand," he said, in a most officious voice. "But perhaps I could spare you a few moments."

I eyed the puzzle.

He cleared his throat.

"Yes, well," he stammered, quickly retrieving the paper and placing it in the bottom drawer. "McHeath."

"Pardon?"

"McHeath, ma'am. Great one for the crosswords, McHeath. Told him not to leave them lying about."

"Yes, of course, Inspector."

After a moment of uncomfortable silence broken only by a useless shuffling about of papers, he plunged right in with the type of remark I should have expected. "And what," he asked, with a light chuckle, "brings the distaff side of the Holmes and Hudson detective agency to my humble office?"

Wouldn't this man ever take me seriously?

"Detective agency? It would appear, Inspector," I coolly responded, "that you are, once more, the possessor of false information. In any event," I added quickly, canceling his opportunity for an added thrust or parry, in this ongoing but self-defeating duel of words, "I thought perhaps you might be interested in this," I stated, placing the packaged statue on his desk.

"What's this?"

"Open it."

The inspector slowly and methodically removed the brown paper wrapping.

"Been out shopping, have you, Mrs. Hudson?" he asked, holding the cherub aloft. "Some sort of gift then, is it?"

I smiled. "A gift? Yes, I suppose you could say that. My gift to the Twillings constabulary. What you are now holding in your hands is what has been up to now the missing murder weapon. The infamous 'blunt instrument' of which you spoke."

"And why am I to believe that?" The question was curtly asked, with the statue being abruptly replaced on the desk.

I shook my head in silent despair. "Inspector Thackeray," I said, with all the earnestness I could muster, "I only wish to contribute in whatever way I can to the many questions that as yet remain unanswered. I'm sure if we could work in tandem, it would only be to the benefit of justice. Now, having said my little speech," I continued, turning the little cherub round so that its back was now toward him, "you will find, once you have the statue clinically examined, that these stains you see are dried blood with fine strands of hair embedded within. Hair, Inspector, that will match, strand for strand, those of the murdered victim."

"Will it indeed, madam?" he queried as his hand slowly twisted the ends of his moustache into tiny points. "Will it, indeed."

About to reach for his pipe, he thought the better of it and, folding his hands atop the desk, leaned forward so that we now faced each other.

"Where did you find the statue?" he asked. "What qualified reason do you have to believe it to be blood, or even, for that matter, the murder weapon itself? You see, Mrs. Hudson," he continued, sinking back into his chair, "if I am to take you seriously, we must approach this in a—"

"I assure you, Inspector," I interjected, "I can answer any and all questions to your utmost satisfaction."

A slight smile began under that moustache

and, for the first time since we met, there was a twinkle in those mousy little eyes. "By gad, Mrs. Hudson," he laughed, good-naturedly, "I believe that you can! But I warn you, madam," he added, lest I think this sudden acquiescence of his had been too quickly obtained, "if you cannot convince me as to your findings, we'll hear no more on the matter, agreed?"

"Agreed."

I then related in detail, with the exception of Vi's astral appearances, the information I had been able to obtain and the events as they had unfolded since my arrival at Haddley; with the earring which I presented to him, and the telling of its discovery in her ladyship's bedchamber, giving added weight to my story. He made no immediate reply when I had finished but sat there lost in thought, tapping the stem of his pipe against the tray. At last, laying it aside, he turned his attention to me.

"The earring, of course, is the one overriding piece of evidence. Without that, Mrs. Hudson, I'm afraid your story would be just that, a story. As to the statue," he continued, noting my questioning glance toward the cherub, "whether the stains are blood or not, remains to be seen. But this," he added, picking up the half-moon clasp, "is something else, again."

He believed me! I sent a silent thank you heavenward.

"Now then, Mrs. Hudson, let us take the circumstances as you have related them, regarding the death of Lady St. Clair."

Seeing I was about to interject, a raised finger bid me to silence as he continued.

"You speak most convincingly of the motives of those whom you believe to be involved. How you came by this knowledge, I don't know. Nor, do I think, I should ask. Nevertheless, what you present me with, ma'am, is no more than overheard conversations. It is not evidence I could take in to a court of law. If death was due to an overdose of chloroform, it is, I'm sorry to say, too late to do anything about it. If we were to exhume the body we'd find nothing. And, in any event, what legal grounds would we have for the ordering of it?"

"Then the murderer goes free?"

"Perhaps not," he replied, toying with the earring.

"Of course, the earring!" I exclaimed. "If the same person committed both—"

"A body," he interrupted, carrying through with my line of thought, "swings as easily at the end of a rope for one murder as two."

"Then it's best," I said, "we turn our attention to the second murdered victim, where we have, at least, a number of loose ends on which to tug."

"Very well put, Mrs. Hudson," he replied. Then withdrawing his pocket watch and holding it in the palm of his hands, I heard him mumble something that sounded like, "One minute late."

"Your watch?" I asked.

My answer appeared in the form of Constable McHeath on entering the office bearing a tray.

"Your tea, Inspector," he said, setting it on

the desk. "I've taken the liberty of bringing an extra cup for you as well, Mrs. Hudson," he added.

"How thoughtful of you, Constable." I smiled.

"Would there be anything else, Inspector?" he asked, with a sideways glance in my direction.

Obviously he had taken the opportunity of tea time to satisfy his curiosity as to the reason for my visit.

"One thing, McHeath," answered Thackeray, as he set about pouring the tea. "Tadlock."

"Sir?"

"Information has come to light that forces me to reevaluate our position with regard to the suspect."

Although it was apparent to all present I was the source of the information, it seemed I was not to be singled out as such. Ah, well.

"The O'Connell girl is now willing to corroborate the lad's story of being with her on the night of the murder, as will her roommate," the inspector stated flatly.

"Changed their story, have they? Perhaps," he added, with an all too obvious accusatory glance toward me, "they've been coerced into doing just that. If you get my meaning, Inspector."

As with his superior, the constable possessed a bureaucratic mind that automatically resisted any attempt to change what had been, up to the time of my arrival, an open and shut case.

"There's more to it than their admission," spoke Thackeray, ignoring the man's inference. "We'll speak of it later at a more convenient time."

"I see," was the obviously annoyed yet controlled response from Thackeray's subordinate. "Will that be all, Inspector?"

"For the moment, yes. Thank you, Mc-Heath."

"Have you made any progress as to the girl's identity?" I asked as the constable closed the door behind him.

"I think we can rule out the idea of her being from Twillings. We've had no reports to date of the disappearance of a girl bearing her description. Still, we may hear something yet."

"Then, no more is known than before?" I asked as the inspector ceremoniously dunked an oatmeal biscuit into his tea.

"Well, yes, one thing," he stated after devouring the biscuit.

"Oh," I asked, leaning forward, "what's that?"

"It seems," he replied, with his eyes avoiding mine, "she was, as you might say, with child."

"Pregnant!"

Inspector Thackeray shifted about uncomfortably in his chair. "That is not a word I would have used in mixed company, Mrs. Hudson. But, yes, she was."

Mixed company! I cast my eyes upward in utter dismay. To converse openly with me of murder and all its sordid implications was deemed quite acceptable by the good inspec-

tor, but by speaking the word applied to an
ongoing process of life, it seemed I had committed the most grievous of social errors. I
could only hope the new century, which
loomed a little more than a year away, would
usher in a more acceptable code of social mo-
res. As it was, I had to contend not only with
the present but with the inspector as well.
And, wishing to enlist his services, I believed
it best to keep my thoughts to myself.

"Do forgive me, Inspector," I apologized, in
demure fashion. "The excitement of the moment, you understand."

His acceptance of my apology went verbally
unacknowledged, with only an inquiry as to
whether I wished more tea.

"Tea? Thank you, no, Inspector," I answered rising from my chair. "I really think I
should be going."

"Then I thank you for coming in, Mrs. Hudson," he replied, easing himself up to a standing position. "Once I've had the results of the
blood test, I shall myself be paying a visit to
Haddley. Possibly sometime tomorrow afternoon. By then," he added, coming round the
desk to escort me to the door, "I'll have a
number of questions I'll want straight answers
to, and I can assure you, they'll not be let off
so lightly this time."

As I turned to leave, I let out an unexpected
gasp.

"Whatever is the matter, Mrs. Hudson?"

"I've completely forgot about poor Will."

"Tadlock?"

"Yes. Surely, Inspector, there's no need now to keep him under lock and key."

"Hmmm, true enough, I suppose," was the admitted but grudgingly given response. "You'll take him back with you, then?"

"Yes, and be glad of the company. Have him meet me down at the livery, would you, Inspector? I've a mare from the estate stabled there."

"God bless you, Mrs. Hudson! I knew you could do it!"

"You'd best save your thanks for a certain Mary O'Connell," I informed my young friend, as we set off on our return trip.

"Know'd Mary would come through, once you explained it all." He grinned, giving quite a professional snap to the reins.

Although now riding as a passenger on the seat beside him, I felt obliged to offer my opinion as to the futility of trying to hasten the horse to that of any speed but her own.

"Weren't tryin' to quicken her pace, missus," the young man informed me, "just seein' to it she don't go falling asleep. When you gets up in years, like ol' Daisy here," he announced, "you tends to tire quicker."

"Do you, now?" I replied, stifling a smile. "I'll have to remember that."

On through the countryside we went, with the lad jabbering merrily away about nothing of any great consequence. Nevertheless, his chattering did provide a well-needed respite from conversations of a darker ilk, to which I'd been subjected over the last few days.

"Do you like singing, Mrs. Hudson?" I was suddenly asked.

"Singing?" I repeated. "Oh, I suppose everyone enjoys a good song, don't they, Will. I don't suppose I'm any exception."

"I mean, do you like to sing?"

"I? Myself? Well, yes, sometimes," I admitted. "Whenever the mood strikes me."

"Sing all the time, I do. Helps makes the time pass, least that's what I think. Ben, though, he's not much of a one for it. Whenever I goes 'bout my chores, he says I sound like a sick bull."

"Is that so!" I exclaimed. "Well, Ben's not here, is he? So sing away, Will Tadlock, if you've a mind to it."

I was then happily entertained with a succession of country airs sung of home and hearth, with an occasional bawdy ballad thrown in for good measure, sung in such an open, innocent, manner, I laughed as heartily as he.

"Why, Will," I announced, "you've a fine voice. And you can tell Ben as much, for me."

"I'll do that then, Mrs. Hudson," he grinned, while giving another flick to the reins. "Now it's your turn."

"My turn?"

"To sing us a song."

"I? Oh, no." I laughed, a trifle embarrassed. "I couldn't. Besides, I can't think of any."

"Must remember one," he said, urging me on with a reassuring smile.

"No," I repeated, "I don't. Oh, there is one

that just popped into my mind. Isn't that the strangest thing? But I don't know if I can remember all the words."

The young lad continued to urge me on.

It seemed I was not to be let off so easily.

Finally, after taking a deep breath, I plunged in, shaking vibrato and all.

> "Goodbye, my sailor boy.
> Farewell, my heart of joy.
> I'll pray each day
> For your safe return.
> Believe me,
> My thoughts will always be
> With you upon the sea.
> So, goodbye, my sailor boy,
> Goodbye."

"Why, Mrs. Hudson," he exclaimed, when I had finished, "that were right good! You'll have to teach—why, missus, what is it? What's wrong?"

I'm afraid I could say or do nothing but stare blankly into space as my thoughts flashed back to a far different locale than this dusty, country road. I saw in my mind's eye a noisy, smoke-filled London music hall and an audience of which I was a part. I could hear that song and see the singer of it. The scene appeared to me as clearly as if viewed through a hand-held stereoscope.

"Will," I managed to blurt out, "we've got to go back!"

"Back? Back where?"

"To Twillings! To the inspector! Right
now!"

"Why, missus, whatever for?"

"Will, please!"

FOURTEEN

Confession

_⚬ϩ~_On seeing Vi emerge from her bedroom, I hurried, as fast as these tired old legs would allow, down the hall to greet her.

"Nora Adams!" I cried out, a bit too impulsively, I'm afraid. Nonetheless, I was hard pressed to contain myself.

"Who?" she asked, startled by my descent upon her.

"Nora Adams!" I repeated.

"And who might she be, when she's at home?" asked my old friend, eyeing me up and down as if I'd gone completely mad.

Clutching her hands in mine, I beamed, "I know who she is!" And, in my excitement, I confess I literally pulled her back into the bedroom before flinging the door shut behind me.

"Do you, dear? That's nice, isn't it?" she answered, in an overly soothing tone. "Why don't you sit down and relax, there's a luv, and I'll have Dr. Morley . . ."

"Oh, Vi." I laughed. "I haven't taken leave

of my senses, though I suppose it must look that way. But, at a time like this," I continued, now pacing the floor, "it's not easy to appear as cool and collected as would a certain detective I could mention."

"At a time like what?" she asked, joining me step for step in my never-ending path around the room.

"Vi!" I exclaimed in annoyance. "There's hardly room for the both of us to pace, now is there?"

"Shall we take turns, then?"

I made a wry face.

The problem was solved by sitting ourselves down in two chairs beside the grate.

"There, that's better, ain't it?" she smiled. "Now, let's hear what you've been gettin' yourself so all worked up about."

"Our unknown murder victim," I began, moving my chair in a little closer to the warmth of the fire, "was none other than Nora Adams!"

"Nora—? I don't—?"

"No, of course you don't, dear," I answered, in response to her puzzled expression. "The girl is, or was, up until the time of her death, the toast of the London music halls. It was she who introduced the song all London is singing, 'Goodbye, My Sailor Boy.' "

"You're sayin' that young thing what were lyin' out there," she announced, indicating direction with a turn of her head toward the window, "was one of them fancy music hall entertainers? Cor! That does add a bit of spice to it, don't it? I mean, what with her bein' on the stage and all." Her eyes fairly sparkled at the thought of it. "So, how'd you find out about this here Nora Adams? From the inspector?"

"Certainly not!" I responded, most indignantly. "I realized it for myself when coming back from Twillings with young Will Tadlock. And quite an enjoyable ride it was, too. We were singing songs, you see, and—"

"Singing songs! What, you?"

I ignored the fact she expressed more surprise in finding I had the capacity to lift my voice in song, than she had when I informed her of my discovery of the dead girl's identity, and blithely carried on. "When Will asked if I knew any songs, the tune 'Sailor Boy,' popped into my head. Halfway through the chorus of the song it suddenly struck me where I had heard it and who it was that had sung it. But in all honesty, I have to admit I've only myself to blame for not remembering all this earlier."

"You knew her, then?"

"No, but I'd seen her, you see, not more than a month ago at the Empress with Mrs. Waddell, an old friend from down the street. But from where we sat, the girl's features were not all that clear. Besides," I added, thinking back a good many years ago when Vi and I would make a night of it, "you remember what music halls are like."

"Still as poorly lit and smoky as ever, are they?" she asked, bending over to retrieve a poker beside the grate.

"Worse, if anything," I replied. "Mind you, it's not that I'm trying to make excuses for myself, but viewing that poor dead girl's remains is quite a different matter from seeing her costumed-up and prancing about onstage."

"Well, 'course it is, I should say!" Vi agreed reassuringly as she set about poking through the ashes. "And the inspector knows all about this here Nora, does he?"

"Oh, yes," I answered. "I informed the inspector after I had Will return me to the police station. Which is why I'm a little later than I thought I'd be."

I then related to Vi my meeting with Thackeray and that gentleman's less than favorable response to the release of young Tadlock, but nevertheless, I added, with justifiable pride, with the information and physical evidence I had presented to him, I could now state we had ourselves an ally in Inspector Jonas Thackeray. When I mentioned that the murdered victim had been with child at the time of death, I received the following reaction: "Pregnant!"

I tsk-tsk'd the word. "Really, Violet!"

"What? What'd I say?"

"Nothing dear." I smiled. "A private joke."

Too absorbed in her own thoughts with all she had heard, she let it pass.

"Well, that lets Lady Big-Wig off the hook. Can't blame her for that, at least. 'Course, that's not to say she couldn't have done away with the girl, if she found Sir Charles had been up to—you know."

"You think the baronet was involved in some sort of sordid affair with the Adams girl?"

"Could be. Why not, eh? Then again, with that bunch you never know. With the exception of Dr. Morley, of course."

"Dr. Morley?"

"Aye. He's the only one of the lot that doesn't seem to have a motive."

"None that you've heard," I countered.

"No, not our Dr. Morley," she stated most adamantly. "As nice a man as ever there was. And a good lookin' one at that. No, not the type, you see."

"Why, Violet Warner," I answered in response with a laugh, "I do believe you're sweet on our doctor!"

"Sweet!" she exclaimed, straightening up in her chair, with hands making nervous little adjustments to her collar. "Why, I never heard of such a thing! You must be daft!"

"Just teasing," I smilingly consoled her, with a pat to her hand and a tactful change of subject. "You remember telling me what a good ear you have for music?"

"What's this all about, now?"

"I've a tune I'd like you to hear."

"You're not going to sing, are you?"

"Tell me if you recognize this," I said, ignoring her barbed remark.

I had no sooner begun humming when Vi broke in by remarking, " 'Course I do. You heard me humming it the other night. It's the same one I've heard Sir Charles plunkin' away at," she answered, quite pleased with herself.

"Exactly," I replied. "And although I didn't realize it 'til this afternoon, *that* tune, my dear

Violet, is none other than 'Goodbye, My Sailor Boy.' "

Her pleased expression quickly faded. "What! The same tune as your Nora Adams? But how could Sir Charles—?"

The question was not to be answered, for at that very moment my eye had caught a shadow that lay between floor and door, with its source originating from the outside hall. I alerted Vi by making pointed gestures toward the door while mouthing the words, "Someone—is—listening—outside."

Her reaction was to reach down and grasp the poker that lay beside the grate, and together we cautiously made our way forward. With Vi at the ready with poker tightly clutched and held in a defensive position over her head, I reached for the handle and, flinging the door open, was confronted by a white walrus moustache. Behind the drooping foliage stood a shaken Colonel Wyndgate.

"Good heavens, madam! What do you intend to do with that!" he sputtered, eyeing the upraised poker.

"Never mind that, what were you doin' outside the door!" demanded Vi. "Inspectin' the wood for termites?"

"Inspecting the—! My dear woman," he fumed with jowls a-wagging, "I've no idea what you're talking about!"

"But you *were* standing outside the door, Colonel. Why?" I asked.

"Why? Why, Mrs. Hudson? I simply, that is to say—" he sputtered before regaining his composure. "I was just on my way downstairs

when I thought I'd stop and ask for the plea-
sure of accompanying you ladies to dinner.
Never had so much as a time to knock,
when—"

"Well, it's queer you've never asked before!" snapped an unconvinced Violet.

"And I jolly well doubt that I ever shall
again!" growled the beet-red face.

"You can put the poker down, Vi." I smiled.
"I think we're safe, for the present. And," said
I, turning to the old soldier, "since we *are* fam-
ished and since it *is* dinner time, Colonel, we'd
be only too happy to accompany you."

With respect to those around the table, the
conversation, while restrained, was nevertheless amiable. Gone from the dining table were
the underlying tensions that prevailed when
last I sat amongst them. It appeared as if they
were trying to put the events of the last few
days behind them. While praiseworthy in itself, it would prove to be before night's end
somewhat premature.

After expressing my compliments on the
meal to Lady Margaret, while secretly hiding
the remaining portions of an all too rubbery
Yorkshire pudding under my mashed pota-
toes, I turned my attention to the baronet.

"Dr. Morley is not joining us tonight, Sir
Charles?"

"Not this evening, Mrs. Hudson. He left
word that he was feeling a trifle under the
weather, I'm afraid."

"Perhaps he should see a doctor!" guffawed
the old colonel.

From around the table a small and embarrassing polite ripple of laughter followed.

"More wine, Margaret?"

"Yes, perhaps I will, Henry."

Hogarth, who had been standing silently to the back of Sir Charles's chair, was at her side in an instant.

"Ladies?" A questioning look from the younger St. Clair.

"No more for me, Squire," spoke Vi.

"Nor I," I replied, executing a conspiratorial kick to my companion's foot in the hope she would voice no objection when I announced, once more, on rising, "Again, a lovely meal, Lady Margaret. Now if everyone will excuse us?"

On taking our leave from the table, I caught Hogarth's attention with a nod of my head toward the door. He took my meaning by answering in kind with a slight and silent nod of his own.

Once outside, I turned to Vi. "When they retire to the music room, how do they occupy their time?" I asked.

"Well, they usually all retire to the music room. Sir Charles might play the piano. Lady Margaret does a bit of needlework. Squire and Colonel might read for a while before headin' off for a game of cards."

"And their length of stay within the room, would be—?"

" 'Bout an hour at best, I should say. Why'd you ask?"

"I want you to take yourself down to the music room and await their arrival," I stated, ignoring her question. "Keep them company until I can join you."

"They'll love that, I'm sure. And where are you off to then, eh?"

"To see Dr. Morley," I answered. "I want to find out just how much under the weather he is. I hadn't expected him not to show for dinner."

She stepped back with a questioning look. " 'Ere, now, you're up to summat, you are. What's this all about?"

Before I had time to respond, Hogarth, on taking his leave of the dining room, closed the door behind him and approached. "You wanted to see me, Mrs. Hudson?" he whispered in a most confidential tone.

From the gleam in his eyes, I could see he was quite caught up in being part of a secret triumvirate.

"Yes, Hogarth, I do," I answered, drawing him in closer. "Inspector Thackeray will be arriving at the back entrance within the hour. It's important no one knows of his arrival, save Mary."

"I understand perfectly, madam," he replied, trying to contain his excitement. "Is there anything particular you wish me to do?"

"Just give him whatever assistance you can," I replied. "If all goes as planned, we should end this mystery tonight. If not, I'm afraid I'll look the complete fool."

"Never you worry, Mrs. Hudson, all will go well," was the venerable gentleman's reassuring and emphatic response. "But I must get back. They'll be wondering, you see. Good luck," he whispered, closing the door behind him.

"And now, perhaps you'd like to tell *me* just what is going on!" exclaimed an irate Violet with foot a-tapping in a show of frustrated annoyance.

"I'm sorry, Vi, but there just isn't time," I answered, casting a wary eye toward the dining room door. "They could be out here any minute. Please, just go along with what I've asked."

"Right then," was the tight-lipped reply. "But if I was Dr. Watson . . ." Mumbling away to herself, she turned on her heels and flounced off down the hall.

While I sympathized inwardly for my old friend, there had been precious little opportunity, since my arrival back from Twillings, to present her with the answers to the many questions that, until now, had remained a puzzle.

Daisy's agonizingly slow plodding gait had turned out to be a blessing in disguise, affording me, as it did, ample time to slowly but surely mentally tie all the loose ends together into one neat package. While I readily admit there were still certain aspects of the case I would have to leave to conjecture, I remained wholly convinced I now held in my head the why, how, and by whom of it.

"Dr. Morley?"
No answer.
With the door being slightly ajar, I gave it a push and, poking my head round the corner,

called out again. "Dr. Morley, are you all right?"

"Ah, Mrs. Hudson, is it? Please, come in."

I stepped into a sparsely furnished room, with the only source of light emanating from the fireplace. Two wing-back chairs, one of which he occupied, sat before the dancing flames as shadowy fingers flickered 'cross his face. A whiskey decanter, placed on a small end table beside the chair, caught the fire's glow within its cut-glass prism, producing silent explosions of color.

With one hand tightly clutching his drink, I was waved by the other into the chair opposite.

"Sir Charles tells us you're not feeling well," I remarked, taking my place in the chair.

A slight trace of a smile appeared. "Still the lady with an inquisitive bent for all things medical, I see," he remarked, in reference to our first meeting, adding with a slight pat to his stomach, "The truth is, I suffer from nothing more than a mild case of dyspepsia, Mrs. Hudson. Still, I appreciate your concern."

"I thought perhaps you might be suffering instead from a guilty conscience," I replied in manner calm.

There was no appreciable response, nor so much as a raised eyebrow. His only reaction was to refill his glass before stating simply, with little or no emotion, "You know, don't you?"

I nodded. "Yes, Dr. Morley, I do."

"I surmised as much the morning Mrs.

Warner spoke of the chloroform. But I couldn't be sure. Did you know then?"

"No, not really," I confessed. "But it did occur to me the only one with ready access to the chemical would be a doctor. What sent me off course was so much had been applied. From what I could gather, it seemed a far greater amount had been used than what normally—"

"That was not due to any medical error on my part," he cut in sharply. "There was a struggle you see, the bottle spilled—"

"Dr. Morley," I sputtered, "this isn't a case of malpractice but one of murder!"

"What? Oh, yes, I see what you mean. A doctor's ego speaking, Mrs. Hudson." Then in mockingly dramatic tones he stated, "Accuse a physician of anything but unprofessionalism, madam, even if it includes the taking of a life."

"I find your humor to be in bad taste," I stated coldly.

"You're right, of course, Mrs. Hudson. A joke as sick as the doctor, it seems."

He groaned slightly.

"You *are* sick!"

"It's nothing. It will pass, shortly."

He brought the glass to his lips but instead of downing the drink, merely sipped at it.

"One question, madam."

"Yes?"

"How in the world did Mrs. Warner know someone was in the room?"

It was a question I hadn't prepared myself for. My mind spun madly around like miniature cogwheels, until at last clicking into place with the appropriate response. "Does that really matter now?" I asked.

A resigned sigh on his part. "No, I suppose not," he answered.

A relieved sigh on my part.

Except for an occasional crack from the burning logs, a period of silence followed.

"I've been such a fool," he muttered at last, staring deep into the flames. "I can see that now. I don't even know why I did it. No," he said, returning his gaze to me, "even that's a lie. I know all too well."

"As do I," I quietly remarked. "Although at first, I wondered how a man, whose whole career was devoted to the care and cure of others, could possibly find it within himself to take a life. The motive, I concluded, must have been a powerful one, indeed. You are not a rich man, are you, Doctor?"

There was an embarrassed shuffling of his feet coupled with a movement of his hand in the covering of a frayed cuff.

"I'm sorry," I said, "but your attire tells me as much."

"No, Mrs. Hudson," he responded, reaching over to empty the remaining contents of the decanter into his glass, "I'm not a rich man. Standing, yes; prestige, yes. But money, no. Dr. Thomas Morley, personal physician to the house of Haddley," he proclaimed, holding his glass on high, as if it were a banner. "Has a fine ring to it, does it not, madam? A verbal calling card, as it were, affording me a preferred table and service at our finest eating establishments, as well as the honor of serving as a member on various social committees at the local level."

He slowly lowered his glass.

"But bear in mind, dear lady," he continued, "this is not a large community and my practice is small. One does not grow rich from social standing."

"But," I countered, "it appears you have a comfortable life and the demands on your time cannot be that great. Why this obsessive need for money?"

He leaned that handsome face forward, throwing his arms out in an expansive gesture.

"Do I look like the kindly old country doctor? Ah, but London, that's a different matter entirely."

"London?"

"With the right amount of capital, Mrs. Hudson, I could buy my own practice. Set myself up in a fashionable district and attend to the ailments, real or otherwise, of the elite."

"And so," I said, "you were offered money to dispose of her ladyship with, no doubt, an added incentive of introductions to all the right people."

"Yes. True enough."

Before I could add anything more he clutched his stomach and bit his lower lip in reaction to the pain.

"Dr. Morley!" I cried out. "Please, let me get you something!"

He waved aside my offer, sinking back even further in his chair.

The heat from the fire was making it far too

uncomfortable for me and, had I the strength, I would have moved the chair. As it was, I sat there waiting until he had regained his composure before asking, "And how much were you to be paid for disposing of *me*?"

He avoided my eyes and, indirectly, my question, with one of his own. "You knew it was me, then?"

"In retrospect, yes," I answered. "There was one single incident that stood out above all else."

"Yes?" And that was—?"

"The taking of my pulse as I lay on the floor. It was, if you'll pardon a play on words, Doctor, a dead giveaway."

"Yes, I see what you mean." A heavy sigh and a dejected shake of the head followed. "But, you're wrong on one point, Mrs. Hudson. There was no money involved. I decided on my own to dispose of you. A matter of self-preservation, as it were. You seemed to be everywhere, asking too many questions of too many people. And when you stayed behind, rather than attend the funeral, even that made me suspicious. Later that same day, I inspected the room upstairs and found a fresh set of woman's footprints. I knew they had to be yours. At that point, everything seemed to be falling apart. Everything."

He buried his face in his hands as his body heaved in anguish and remorse.

"But, you, yourself, were not responsible for the young girl's death," I quietly remarked.

"No," he acknowledged, as hands came down to reveal red-rimmed eyes, "but if I had made known who was responsible, it would have only resulted in my part in her ladyship's death. What a mess I've made of my life," he added, in a voice cracking in emotion. "What an utter, utter mess."

This was not the Dr. Morley Violet would have recognized. This was a man broken in spirit by his actions. A man I could feel neither anger nor contempt for, merely pity.

"But as for my attempt on your life, Mrs. Hudson, you must believe me," he implored, with eyes searching mine for some sign of absolution, "I'm truly sorry it ever happened. No one is more grateful than I that you are still alive."

"One other person, I think, Dr. Morley."

A sad and knowing smile. "Yes, of course," he replied after taking yet another sip from his drink before continuing.

"I want to tell you a secret," he said very quietly and with obvious sincerity. "Although, it's possible on hearing it you may think me quite mad. But something happened to me that night. Something I can only describe as being in the nature of a deeply profound religious experience. As I stood over you in that darkened room, a light appeared before me. A light of iridescent blue emanating from a figure that stood before me. It was an angel, madam. An angel sent from heaven."

Good God, he was speaking of Violet!

"I knew it must be a sign. I rushed from her ladyship's chamber and, returning to my room, fell down on my knees in prayer. But with heaven itself intervening to condemn what I had done, what hope had I for salvation?"

"Dr. Morley," I interrupted, "I think it only fair to warn you Inspector Thackeray will be arriving at any minute, if he is not here already. I shall have no other choice but to tell him of our conversation."

"You do that, Mrs. Hudson," he answered, with a tired sigh. "As for myself, dear lady, I believe it is now time I took my leave."

He downed the remaining contents of his glass in one gulp before the horrible realization of what he had done became all too apparent to me.

"Dr. Morley!" I screamed, pushing myself up out of the chair.

He doubled over grasping both arms around his stomach and, in his attempt to rise, swayed dizzily from side to side as his now glazed eyes swept wildly about the room. The body fell awkwardly back into the chair as involuntary spasms continued to jerk the lifeless form about like a stringed puppet. Then just as quickly as it had begun, it was over.

Shaken, I closed the door behind me and headed downstairs, leaving Dr. Morley and his confession to a higher authority.

FIFTEEN

Conclusion

∼AFTER A FEW hurried and private words with Hogarth in the downstairs hall, I entered the music room to find all engaged, as Vi had so aptly described they would be, in their customary nightly routine—with the exception of Sir Charles, who sat not at the piano, but on a silk damask sofa, thumbing idly through the pages of a book.

Though all eyes were turned in my direction as I made my entrance, Violet was the only one thoughtful enough to greet me on my arrival. "There you are, luv. I was wonderin' what was keeping you."

Her voice startled the old colonel, who had been indulging himself in an after-dinner nap. As I passed by him to take my seat alongside Vi, he stirred himself long enough to inquire as to the health of Dr. Morley.

"He's at rest," I answered simply and all too truthfully.

"I was hoping he'd be well enough to put

in an appearance," spoke the squire, extracting a cigarette from its case. "If the colonel keeps drifting off I shall be in need of someone later on for a hand or two at cards."

The old soldier mumbled something or other and promptly fell back to sleep.

"I understand you made a visit to Twillings this afternoon, Mrs. Hudson," spoke Lady Margaret, without raising her eyes from the needle that darted in and out of her embroidery.

"Twillings? Actually, I did, yes," was my startled and stumbling reply, hoping that would be an end to it.

The needle came to a stop as the eyes of Lady Margaret slowly lifted and focused questioningly on me, waiting for a continuance.

What now? I knew I had better come up with some sort of follow-up. I couldn't always rely on Violet to step in—though I sensed she felt as uncomfortable as I with the situation, for she began making odd little noises in her throat.

"My shawl," I blurted out.

"Yes?"

"Ah, yes, my shawl," I repeated. "I'm in desperate need of a new one, actually. I thought perhaps I'd see something in the village, but no luck, I'm afraid."

"Pity."

Nothing more was said. The baronet's wife hadn't believed a single word of what I'd said. I felt like a fool.

Everyone quietly returned to their own private thoughts until I at last gathered up courage to put forward the following request. "I understand you play the piano, Sir Charles. Perhaps you'd honor us with a tune or two."

"I'm afraid I'm not—"

"Oh, come now, old boy," his younger brother broke in, "you know you were just waiting to be asked."

"Something by Scarlatti would be nice, Charles," suggested the lady of the manor.

Sir Charles obligingly took his seat at the piano. As the melody flowed from the glistening rosewood instrument, a dramatic backdrop for both pianist and piano was provided by three windows that swept from floor to ceiling. Outside, the moon shyly edged its way in and out of blue-gray clouds illuminating, at various intervals, an audience of elms swaying in the night wind, as if in rhythm to the music from within.

When the cantata was finished a smattering of applause followed, with the baronet turning in our direction to ask, "Perhaps the ladies would care for something a little more modern?"

"Would you know 'Goodbye, My Sailor Boy'?" I asked.

"'Goodbye . . . '?" He pursed his lips in thought for a moment or two. "No, I don't believe I do, Mrs. Hudson."

"'Course you do, Sir Charles," Vi chimed in, giving a knowing nudge to my side. "Why, I've heard you play it myself on more than one occasion. Goes like this." At which point she proceeded to lah-lah-lah the tune.

"Oh, that one! By Jove, I do! Quite popular

in London right now. Never was quite sure of the title. You must have heard it as well, Henry."

The squire, coming round to the side of the piano with glass in hand, fortified himself with another drink before stating, "Can't say that I have, old boy."

The first few notes had no sooner begun when a voice from the moonlit grounds outside could be heard accompanying the piano in song.

As Sir Charles continued playing, albeit haltingly, we who were sitting rose to our feet and moved toward the window. Though not a word was spoken, puzzled, questioning, and frightened glances were exchanged by all present.

The clouds had parted, allowing a shaft of moonlight to make visible on the outside grounds the solitary, ghostlike figure of a young woman.

Completely unnerved as the rest by the apparition, Sir Charles abandoned the piano to join us at the window. The singing continued in a hauntingly clear voice as the shadowy form of a young woman glided in closer, allowing those of us within the room a horrifying view of her blood-stained face.

Lady Margaret promptly fainted.

Both the colonel and Sir Charles stood rooted to the spot like waxworks in a Madame Tussaud setting. Vi stumbled back, clutching the piano for support. The squire, his face contorted in horror and disbelief, flung his heavy crystal glass toward the window with such force its impact sent shards of window glass flying outward.

"It's Nora! It's Nora!" he screamed out, over and over again.

"How could it be Nora!" I demanded of him. "You killed her!"

"Yes, but you saw her—we all did!" he shot back before realizing the gravity of his admission.

He returned to the liquor cabinet where his shaking hands tried with partial success to fill a whiskey glass.

I whirled toward his brother. "Sir Charles," I commanded the man, "please see to your wife, she's fainted!"

Still in a somewhat dazed condition himself, the baronet, with an assist from the colonel, helped the woman onto the sofa.

"Emma Hudson, just what is goin' on here!" Vi cried out, quite visibly upset with all she had witnessed. "First a ruddy ghost singing songs as nice as you please outside the window, then the squire confessin' to murder—I thought we were after—" She shot a glance toward Sir Charles but held her tongue in check.

"I think it's Henry who has the explaining to do," answered the baronet, leaning over his wife as he attempted to revive her with gentle taps to the cheek.

The eyes of Lady Margaret slowly fluttered open. "What is it, Charles?" she asked. "What's happened?"

"It seems, old darling, brother Henry has just confessed to one and all of having murdered the young woman they found outside."

"Well, what of it!" snapped the younger man, throwing back his drink. "Who's going to send me off to the gallows? You, Charles? You, Margaret? What about you, Colonel?"

"What! What! Well, really, old boy—that is . . ."

"No," responded the squire haughtily, "I thought not! And," he added, turning on Vi and me, "who's going to believe two foolish old women? The reappearance of Nora from the dead would only add to the absurdity of the claim. But you go ahead, Mrs. Hudson," he continued, with a certain arrogance to his voice, "run off to your inspector. I can well imagine the reaction your story will receive."

"Can you indeed, sir?"

All eyes turned to the door as Thackeray, sans bowler, strode into the room.

"You heard, Inspector?"

"Indeed I did, Mrs. Hudson. I'm sorry, Squire, but I must formally charge you in the murder of Nora Adams."

"Nora St. Clair, Inspector," I corrected him.

A moment of stunned silence was followed in turn by several gasps of astonishment.

"St. Clair? How'd you mean, madam?" asked Thackeray.

I turned my attention to the squire of Haddley. "Shall I tell them, or will you?"

"You seem to have all the answers," he remarked bitterly, sinking down into a chair.

"Well, I'd like to know how you knew it was the squire," stated Violet. "And what's all this Nora St. Clair business, eh?"

"In answer to your first question, Vi," I replied, "you remember me telling you of having learned that the baronet and his wife as well as the squire returned to the estate unexpectedly?"

"Aye."

"Both Sir Charles and Lady Margaret were seen by Hogarth and the staff on their arrival. Only the squire's reappearance went unnoticed until the next morning. He was the only one who could have brought Nora to Haddley without anyone's knowledge."

"Why? For what purpose?" queried Sir Charles.

"Why, indeed? It was a question I repeatedly asked myself. The idea of bringing a mere slip of a girl from the London stage back here for some sort of tête-a-tête would have been mad. Although he assumed, Sir Charles, that both you and her ladyship would be away, your mother was still here and very much alive at the time. No, it had to be the girl's idea. Lady Margaret," I asked, "what would you say if I told you your dead niece was a music hall entertainer, unmarried, and with child?"

"Good God!"

"Yes." I smiled. "That would have been the exact response from her ladyship."

"Then it must have been blackmail!" exclaimed Vi.

"Exactly," I answered. "Which brought me back to my original supposition that the dead girl could only have been his daughter. No doubt, she sent the squire a letter telling him she wanted to see him. When he arrived in London, she demanded money to keep what she had become from being made known. Am I right so far, Squire?"

I took his silence as an affirmation.

"But," his brother broke in, "Henry is completely without funds. How could he——?"

"If you would allow a supposition on my part, I believe he hoped to get the money from her ladyship by concocting some sort of story of needing it to pay off his gambling debts. He certainly wasn't going to reveal the real reason. The fact that Nora willingly accompanied him back here, for I cannot imagine he dragged her to Haddley by force, indicates to me the daughter knew all too well she had little hope of her father sending her the money by post."

"Then, what you are saying is, she returned with Henry to get the money rather than wait in London for the promise of it," Lady Margaret said in a questioning tone. "But that's impossible!" she suddenly announced, quite emphatically. "We saw no girl here."

"A makeshift room on the top floor, m'lady," answered the inspector. "She stayed there."

"I see," she responded softly, accompanying her words with a pitiful shake of that patrician head. "And your wife, Henry, what's become of her?" she asked.

"Died in Australia five years ago," the squire snapped.

"But I say!" announced the colonel to one and all. "All this talk about a daughter blackmailing her own father—never would have happened in my day!"

"But remember, Colonel Wyndgate," I reminded him, "she and her mother had been abandoned by the father and were left to make a life of their own abroad. The stage would have been one of the few things left open to her when her mother died. No doubt the knowledge she was expecting a child prompted her return to England to see that the child would be properly taken care of financially—the only way she knew how, by blackmail."

"Well, I doubt very much," was Sir Charles's comment to his brother, "if you had any luck getting money from mother, old boy, whatever the reason."

"Not so much as a farthing!" was the embittered response.

"Not even after what I imagine would have been an impassioned plea from Nora when paying a call on your mother in her bedroom," I added.

I received a most surprised look from the squire. "How did you know that?"

"Why, Em here found the girl's earring in her ladyship's room." Violet beamed proudly. "Ain't that right, luv?"

"Vi, please. You were saying, Squire?"

"When I went upstairs to see Nora, after being turned down by mother, I told her she would just have to be patient. I'd give what I could when I could. Later that same night, she told me she had burst into her ladyship's room, revealing the whole story, and demanded money to keep her silence. The up-shot of it all was that I was now to be cut out of the will entirely. Whether Mother would have or not, I don't know—but I couldn't take the chance."

"It was then you brought Dr. Morley into the whole sorry affair," I broke in, "with the offer of payment to do away with her lady-ship."

"Not Dr. Morley!" gasped my old friend.

"I'm sorry, Vi, but it's true. The doctor him-self testified as much to me."

"But why would the squire want to kill Nora?" she asked. "I mean, what with her la-dyship dead before she could change the will, and all."

"I can only assume," I stated, "that after the daughter learned of the death the price went up considerably."

"It was her greed that did Nora in!" the squire suddenly blurted out.

"No, Squire," I retorted. "It was *you* who did her in! She wanted more money. There was an argument. You struck her on the head with the first thing that came to hand—a small marble statuette."

"I might mention," added the inspector, "the statue of which Mrs. Hudson speaks is now in the hands of the coroner to be ana-lyzed."

"And after killing her," I pressed on, "you dressed her in her coat and dragged the body outside in the belief that, when found, she'd be mistaken for a local girl from Twillings. On hearing the voices of Will and Mary on the grounds, you abandoned your victim and beat a hasty retreat back to Haddley."

I received no reply, there being little need for one in any event.

Drawing the inspector aside, I informed him of Dr. Morley's suicide. I thought it best, for the moment, to keep the death confidential. As Vi had taken the doctor's role in the murder of Lady St. Clair to heart, I had no wish to upset her even further with this added revelation.

"I say, madam," spoke the colonel, lumbering his bulk toward me, "who the devil are you, anyway? Some sort of a detective?"

"Mrs. Hudson," the inspector answered for me, "is a cohort of the famous Sherlock Holmes, Colonel Wyndgate."

The old soldier was left momentarily speechless. "Sherlock Holmes! Good heavens." He gasped. "Inspector! Shouldn't you have the woman under lock and key?"

"What in the world are you talking about?" asked a thoroughly bewildered Thackeray.

"I mean to say," he spluttered, "this, this, Sherlock Holmes fellow—isn't he the chap that went about murdering those poor women in London a few years back?"

"Colonel Wyndgate!" I exploded in laughter. "I believe you're confusing Mr. Holmes with Jack the Ripper!"

"What! What! Yes, well, Sherlock, Ripper, always did get those two mixed up."

The colonel's faux pas did, at least, lighten the mood until Lady Margaret, walking slowly toward the shattered window, asked plaintively, of no one in particular, "Are we now to be haunted the rest of our lives by the ghost of Nora St. Clair?"

"I believe I can put your mind to rest on that score, m'lady," I answered. "Inspector Thackeray?"

"You may come in now," he called out, turning his attention toward the door.

In stepped Mary O'Connell.

Still wearing Nora's coat and with hair that now hung down to her shoulders, she entered nervously, wiping the "blood" from her face.

"Why, it's our Mary!" exclaimed Vi.

"Good Lord!" gasped Lady Margaret. "One of the servants!"

"Explain yourself, sir!" Sir Charles demanded of the inspector.

"It would appear, old boy," announced the squire on the inspector's behalf, "our ghost was nothing more than a cheap theatrical trick. Still," he added, affecting a mocking bow from the waist, "my compliments, Mrs. Hudson. You did stage the production, I take it?"

I answered with a slight smile and a nod of the head.

"Why, Mary," cried Violet, rushing to the girl, "you've got blood all over you!"

"It was nothin' more than Cook's tomato sauce," she answered with a mischievous grin.

"You weren't hurt by the glass, were you, dear?" I asked. "I'm afraid that was something I hadn't counted on."

"It gave me more of a fright than anything else, Mrs. Hudson."

"Yes, well, you did just fine, Mary," Thackeray said smiling. "You best run along now, and get cleaned up."

"And, Mary," I added, "don't worry about a probable loss of your position. Mr. Holmes has many influential friends. I'm sure something can be arranged for both you and Will."

She grasped both my hands in hers, started to speak, then, as if fearing she would become too emotional, rushed out of the room.

By mid-morning the next day, Mrs. Warner and I were on a train heading back to London.

"Well, you can feel right proud of yourself, Emma Hudson," announced my companion with a smile as we settled ourselves down on opposite seats.

"Don't be too hasty in discounting your own contribution," I smiled back.

"Aye," she bubbled over in girlish enthusiasm, "we make quite a pair, don't we? Can't wait, I can't, to tell your Mr. Holmes all about it."

"Oh."

"Why, what's the matter, luv?"

"It's just that, well, I shouldn't mention anything if I were you to Mr. Holmes or Dr. Watson, for that matter, about your ability to—"

"Flit off?"

"Yes"—I chuckled—"flit off. In fact," I added, "it's best we keep that entire aspect of the case to ourselves."

"What they don't know won't hurt 'em, is that it?"

"Quite."

Steel wheels continued to click past a never-ending countryside where a light powdered snow did its best to cover the naked fields of November. A small boy at a level crossing flung his arms about in a cheery wave as we whooshed by. I managed to return the wave with a smile from behind a smudged window.

"What are your plans then, after we gets back to London?"

"What?"

"Sorry, luv. Didn't mean to startle you."

"No, that's quite all right," I answered. "Just daydreaming. My plans?" I said, picking up her question. "How'd you mean?"

"Well, I was thinkin' maybe we could start out on our own, in this here detective business."

"Would you have me give Mr. Holmes and Dr. Watson their notice?" I responded light-heartedly.

"No, nothing like that," she answered, quite seriously. "We could do it part time, like. Doubt if we'd be that busy. Maybe the odd case that your Mr. Holmes hasn't time for."

To Vi, it seemed he was still "my" Mr. Holmes.

Although I never openly admitted it to her, to continue on in the role of a private detective was an idea I had been toying with myself. The question now remained whether to enter into a profession containing, as it would, a certain element of danger, or to be satisfied with my lot in the carrying out of simple household chores.

"It's something to think about," was my

noncommittal reply as I returned my gaze to the window.

"About Mary," spoke Vi, breaking my reverie, "how did she get Nora's coat?"

"Still on that, are you?" I smiled.

"Well, it's like you say, ain't it? I just want to tie all the loose ends up in me mind."

"From the inspector," I answered. "After returning to Twillings the second time with Will, I fashioned together for the inspector the scene to be played out by Mary. After some gentle persuasion on my part, he agreed to go along with the idea. If I was to pass her off as the dead girl's ghost, I'd need Nora's coat, at least, to set the stage, as it were. I'm sorry I couldn't let you in on the charade, Vi, but I needed an honest reaction from you when Mary as Nora put in her appearance."

"Aye, well, you got that all right. Thought I'd drop dead meself when she showed up. But as to the coat," she continued, harking back to her original query, "the inspector brought it with him when he showed up later that night, right?"

"Exactly. And," I added, "on my return, earlier that same afternoon, I went to Mary with my plan. After informing her of Will's release, she was only too glad to assist in any way she could."

"And if I knows Emma Hudson, it was you what arranged her hair like Nora's and taught her that song."

"That's precisely what happened." I smiled. "How perceptive of you, Mrs. Warner."

"Elementary, Mrs. Hudson."

⇌ JILL CHURCHILL ⇌

"Agatha Christie is alive and well and writing mysteries under the name Jill Churchill."

Nancy Pickard

Delightful Mysteries Featuring
Suburban Mom Jane Jeffry

GRIME AND PUNISHMENT
76400-8/$4.99 US/$6.99 CAN

A FAREWELL TO YARNS
76399-0/$5.50 US/$7.50 CAN

A QUICHE BEFORE DYING
76932-8/$4.99 US/$6.99 CAN

THE CLASS MENAGERIE
77380-5/$4.99 US/$5.99 CAN

A KNIFE TO REMEMBER
77381-3/$4.99 US/$5.99 CAN

FROM HERE TO PATERNITY
77715-0/$4.99 US/$6.99 CAN